JUST ANOTHER EPIC ADVENTURE

A SMALL TOWN CAPE COD HOLIDAY ROMANCE

KATIE O'SULLIVAN

Just Another Epic Adventure

Katie O'Sullivan

Copyright 2024 by Katie O'Sullivan.

Cover art design by Michele Hauf

Windmill Point Press

ISBN: 978-1-7354061-4-5

Published in the United States of America

ABOUT THE BOOK

A reality TV star turned reluctant guardian. A single mom who yearns for adventure. Each with a deadline. Can these two help each other get what they want most, in time for Christmas?

Reality TV star Zack Donovan travels the globe seeking danger and his fans eagerly await his outrageous adventures. After a family tragedy makes him the guardian of two small children, the cameras shut off and he rushes home to Cape Cod.

His daredevil lifestyle hasn't exactly prepared him for this, and if he can't prove that he can be a parent the kids' controlling grandmother will demand custody. Does he have to choose between family and career, or can he manage both? Not without some assistance...

Erin Brannigan always lived for the moment – until she found herself pregnant and alone in London. Now she's a single mom, living with her parents and teaching kindergarten on the Cape. She may have crushed on Zack in high school, but the guy is arrogant, obnoxious... and in desperate need of help.

When Zack and Erin reconnect they move quickly from fond memories to mutual distrust. Will first impressions push these two apart or can they find common ground? Both have Christmas deadlines to make life-changing choices... but will the holidays bring them heartache or a happily ever after?

PRAISE FOR KATIE O'SULLIVAN

"Katie O'Sullivan has the unique writing ability to make words and descriptions leap off the page."

Peggy Jaegar, best-selling author

"I've read several books written by Katie O'Sullivan; she is becoming one of my favorite authors. I can't wait to read more of her books."

5-star Amazon review of Battling Benjamin

"Katie O'Sullivan grabs the reader by the lapels and doesn't let go until the last page."

N.N. Light Book Heaven reviews

"O'Sullivan sets her books (yes, I eagerly pre-order each new release) in Cape Cod. I've never been there except through this talented author's words... Highly recommend!"

Claire Marti, USA Today bestselling author

"The author pulls you in and holds your attention right until the very end."

5-star Amazon review of Matt's Mystic Connection

"Sweet with steam Cape Cod story with a happily ever after!... I can watch and read Christmas stories year round. And more during the season. If you like your holiday romances with a bit of steam this is the book for you..."

"There's a lot to love in this sweet and steamy romance. As is her trademark, Katie O'Sullivan takes us to Cape Cod where the holidays are done right. With carols, strolls, house tours and all of the up close and personal family meddling one could want in a small town romance."

For my mom, whose favorite holiday was always Christmas. I miss you always, but especially during the holidays.

PROLOGUE

September
Gaansbai, South Africa

The fifty-foot modified trawler rocked slowly in the undulating ocean, small waves lapping at the hull as the crew weighed anchor near Geyser Rock. Zack Donovan scanned the water's surface and the distant horizon, taking in the brilliant blue skies and calm September waters as a playful breeze tossed his dark curls. He pushed the hair off his forehead and smiled. Conditions couldn't be more perfect than today.

The blue and black neoprene wetsuit felt like a second skin to him. In the last handful of years, he'd been on so many underwater adventures he'd finally given in and bought his own, rather than struggle with the inevitably too-tight fit of the rentals on his wide shoulders and chest. He absolutely hated to feel constricted like that, as if the Universe itself squeezed him in its fist. He'd felt that squeeze one too many times in his life. The custom-fitted wetsuit was an investment he was thankful for every time he pulled it on.

"Hey Zack, you ready for this shoot, man?"

Zack took off his dark sunglasses and turned to his buddy Mike Mullins, standing in the shadow of the pilothouse with his trusty waterproof camcorder already balanced on one shoulder. As tall as Zack but skinny as a rail, his bald head glistened in the morning sun. Mike smiled that crooked smile of his, the one that got them both into trouble and out of it again, depending on the situation. Like Zack, Mike had already donned his wetsuit and looked ready for their upcoming face-to-face with the local residents of these waters.

The other three guys on the film crew were no doubt setting up the on-deck stationary cameras, boom mikes, and soundboard. The team liked to travel light on adventures like this, and Mike captured most of the film that made it onto the show with his portable for that more authentic feel. He was the one who accompanied Zack on the jumps and dives and other crazy stunts that made *Epic Adventures* the popular show that it was.

"Have the rest of the guys changed into their suits yet?" Zack turned back to scan the ocean's surface for fins. Swimming with sharks was always more of an adventure when there were actual sharks in the water with you.

"Four of them have. The other two are making noises like they might change their minds about following through."

Zack shrugged, unconcerned. "Either their buddies will convince them or they'll sit it out. They signed all the paperwork and know that either way the captain won't be giving their money back." And either way would be fine for filming the episode. Viewers loved it when these big talkers ended up backing down from the challenge.

The captain of the boat out of Kleinbaai Harbour was a grizzled hard-ass of a sailor, with a firm no returns policy, whether the customer decided not to enter the water for whatever reason, or even when the sharks were all no-shows. You paid up front for his time, his crew, and his gasoline. Whether or not you actually climbed into the galvanized steel cage and lowered into the shark-infested waters didn't matter to him in the least.

Mike grinned and gestured to his camcorder. "I guess I could also remind them we've already got them on video saying they're psyched for this *epic adventure*. Can't chicken out now." He readjusted the camera, pointing the lens at his friend. "Wanna film the opening now or wait for the guys to join us?"

"We should wait for the guys," Zack said, scanning the horizon again. A large pod of bottlenose dolphins surfaced nearby, arcing out of the water as they raced by. "Hey, can you get them in the shot with me? We could do a quick promo or two."

"Absolutely." Mike adjusted his stance to capture both Zack and the dolphins. "Go."

Zack turned to the camera and gave it his best smile, the one the network loved to put on posters and billboards. "I'm Zack Donovan and this is *Epic Adventures*."

Mike made a rolling gesture with his hand for a few seconds, then said. "And again."

Zack pushed his hair off his forehead and smiled again. "I'm Zack Donovan. Are you ready for our next epic adventure?"

Mike repeated the same rolling hand gesture before saying, "And one more."

"I'm Zack Donovan off the coast of South Africa. And this is *Epic Adventures*."

"Perfect. Nailed it." Mike lowered the camera and jerked a thumb toward the stairwell. "I'll go check on the guys." He turned and headed for the stairs down to the boat's lower level.

The six men changing into wetsuits below deck all worked on Wall Street, financial industry drones looking for that ultimate thrill to brag about over cocktails at their club or at their next college reunion. It was guys like them who made up the majority of Zack's clientele from the very start. Young, freshly minted executives with too much disposable income and not enough excitement in their lives.

From swimming with Great Whites off the coast of South Africa, to helicopter skiing in the mountains of British Columbia, Zack provided that excitement they all yearned for. Over the years, he'd played tour guide to hundreds of groups like this, traveling all over the world for almost every over-the-top adventure imaginable. It never got old for him, that zing of adrenaline pounding through his body that made each new challenge more exciting than the last.

The kind that made him know he was alive.

And for the last few years, the added anticipation of filming the escapades for his weekly TV show, *Epic Adventures*, really got his nerves tingling and his heart racing. Something about sharing those heart-stopping moments with a broader audience made each one even more exhilarating, more dangerous, more immediate. Everything was filmed in one take, no reshoots, as close to an actual live experience as Zack could make it for the viewers at home.

So far on this journey, they'd filmed the group navigating Cape Town International Airport (harrowing in itself for the uninitiated), a brief tour of the city, and then the 160-kilometer drive by chartered van to the harbor this morning, during which Zack and the guys discussed their reasons for being on this adventure. Zack managed to get in a few facts about Great White sharks, trying to dissuade any notion that the creatures were the monsters portrayed on the big screen. Dangerous and wild, yes. Monsters, not so much. The predators preferred to feast on the colony of 60,000 fur seals that called Geyser Rock their home. Zack likened it to an all-you-can-eat buffet in Vegas, which the guys all thought was hilarious.

Although this was Zack's first trip to South Africa, he'd done similar shark tours off the coast of Australia. Most recently, he'd taken three German couples on a tour of the Outback, culminating with diving with Great Whites off the Neptune Islands, Australia's largest fur seal colony. That boat had been higher end than this one, the captain less salty but no less experienced, with champagne and caviar served on the return trip to shore. The current experience was more on the gritty side, from the dusty van ride to the sleepy harbor town to the colorful Afrikaans swearing from the crew... but it seemed to be suiting the Wall Street boys just fine. They'd asked for "real" and this was as authentic as anything Zack could imagine.

And it was going to make a great episode.

Thirty minutes later, the eight men – including the two reluctant ones – were standing inside the steel cage as the winch lowered them into the ocean. Each wore a mask and regulator, the air hoses all hooked to a complicated looking apparatus on the top of the cage, allowing the men to breathe underwater without snorkels or full scuba gear. Three of the men had cameras of their own, determined to take their own underwater photos as proof of their daring.

The water was clear, allowing the bright sun to filter down from the surface. Good light and good visibility meant good video, and Zack gave Mike and his camera lens two enthusiastic thumbs up. Above and to the left, a huge hunk of fish hooked to a long line splashed into the water, a red cloud of blood slowly spreading from the dead carcass. The ocean's current carried the cloud away from the steel cage, giving the men an unobstructed view.

Very quickly the scent of fresh blood lured the first guests closer to the meal, a pair of four-foot-long leopard sharks. They bit at the ragged edges of the dangled fish before coming closer to the cage for further inspection. They circled the steel cage as Mike's camera moved between filming the guys gesturing and taking photos, and the sharks themselves, who soon lost interest in the cage and went back to pulling chunks off the dangled meal.

Having been here before, Zack knew what it meant when, twenty minutes later, the pair raced off like bullets from a gun. *A larger predator is on his way. Finally.* Zack waved to Mike, pointing in the direction where he saw a hulking shadow emerging from the darkness. Seconds later a massive great white drew closer to the cage, easily fifteen feet long if not more, mouth hanging open to show off row upon row of sharp, jagged teeth. It skimmed along right beside them, close but not quite touching the steel as the men inside shrank back as far as possible from the intimidating beast. It circled the meat dangling raggedly from the fishing line, pulling one of the trailing bits clean off before swimming off into the black depths.

The guys in the cage all gestured excitedly to one another, pointing to where the Great White disappeared, maybe thinking the show would soon be over, or that another set of leopard sharks might return.

Zack knew better. The Great White had gotten a taste. He was definitely coming back for the rest.

Sure enough, the majestic beast had circled around somewhere in the darkness, and slowly moved back into their field of vision, making another pass at the dangling meat, this time ripping off half the remaining meat with his powerful jaws before swimming past the cage again, bits of the bloody fish visible in its teeth and trailing from the creature's mouth.

On this second pass, Zack pressed against the galvanized steel of the cage's side, the camera trained on him to capture every move. He reached one arm through the bars as the shark swam close, running his bare hand along its flank. Hard and smooth, more like a pumice stone than sandpaper since his hand was going "with the grain," so to speak. In the back of his mind, he made a mental note to add a bit of narrative about the shark's dermal denticles pointing toward the tail for frictionless swimming, before putting that aside to be in the moment.

What a rush. Close enough to touch one of nature's fiercest predators.

Pulling his arm back into the cage, he turned and flashed a triumphant grin and trademark double thumbs up to the camera and to the rest of the guys, only to notice one of them had slumped to the cage floor. A lump of ill-fitting wetsuit in a heap at the back of the cage. No bubbles discharging from the guy's breathing gear.

Oh shit. Zack's first thought was heart attack, and he slammed the emergency button, sounding the alarms on deck and starting the winch to raise them back to the surface. The Great White took off into the deep. Only when the cage rattled did the other men seem to realize that one of their friends was in trouble, two of them grabbing him under the arms and hauling him into an upright position, his head bobbing ominously from side to side.

Shit shit shit. Tamping down on the panic, Zack wracked his brain to remember if any of the guys indicated health issues on their forms. The top of the cage broke the surface and he could hear the alarm bells ringing through the salt air. The crew leaned over the side of the boat, not knowing the nature of the emergency but ready to help. As they unlatched the door at the top of the cage, Zack ripped off his mask and pointed to the unconscious man. "Pull him up and out first. Quickly. Make sure he's breathing."

Looking back down, he saw the Great White had returned to make another slow pass beneath the floor of the half-submerged cage. And there was Mike on his knees, still fully underwater, still filming the mammoth beast as it did a final observation of the humans before disappearing into the murky depths where sunlight didn't penetrate.

Even as the crew lifted the guy onto the deck, he started to come around. By the time the rest of them were back on board, the sense of emergency fully passed. Chuck was sitting up drinking bottled water, looking pale but smiling and joking with the crew. Apparently, he'd fainted dead away when Zack stuck his arm out through the bars of the cage, thinking he was about to witness a *Jaws* moment up close.

Luckily, Chuck was a good sport about the fact Mike caught the entire thing on film, the passing out and ensuing panic, as well as the good-natured ribbing that followed. The rest of the group agreed it'd been one hell of an adventure, not only the adrenaline rush of being up close and personal with leopard sharks and a Great White, but also the fear induced by their buddy's near-death experience. No one felt they'd been shortchanged or that things ended abruptly because of the health emergency.

They came face to face with a Great White shark, and all lived to tell the tale.

Mission accomplished.

Another *epic adventure* in the books. Or at least on film.

"Well, that was a first," Mike said, stepping up to stand next to Zack at the railing. They'd both changed back into jeans and t-shirts, the harbor slowly coming into view as the trawler made its way to the dock. "For a minute there, I thought the guy keeled over dead."

Zack smiled. "And yet you kept right on filming."

"I was filming the shark, not the dead guy," Mike protested. "That was the biggest Great White I've ever seen up close."

"Yeah, it was pretty impressive."

"And you petted the damn thing, like it was a damn Golden Retriever."

Zack's smile widened. "Hell right I did. Gotta grab those chances when you can. You never know when you'll run out of time."

Mike stared out at the horizon. "I know you've been doing this sort of death-defying stuff longer than the show has been on television. Longer than I've been with you."

"Yeah? And?"

"Is this what you want for the rest of your life? Don't you ever want to settle down? Do the family thing?"

Zack looked away from his friend, staring out across the water. Mike had no clue about Zack's past, and now didn't seem the time for deep discussions. "Never thought about it, honestly. I'm just enjoying the here and now. The adrenaline rush that each new experience brings."

"Have you ever actually lost anyone on one of these adventure trips of yours?"

Zack paused. His smile faded as he looked straight into Mike's eyes. "Not on my trips, no. Crazy as it may sound, safety is always one of my top priorities, for every part of the journey."

"Not on your trips you say," Mike persisted. "But people do die on these sorts of adventures. If not all the time, then a larger than normal percentage of the time."

Zack took a deep breath of salty air and flashed his biggest camera-ready smile. "But not here, not now, and not today." He threw an arm around Mike's shoulder and dragged him toward the back deck of the boat where the Wall Street boys sat drinking celebratory beer. "Let's revel in the here and now, shall we?"

When they drew closer to shore and into range of the local cell tower, notifications began to ping and chime throughout the group. Zack pulled out his cell to see a missed call from his older – and only – sister, Daphne.

He had one more group adventure tour on the calendar – an African safari on a Kenyan preserve for some Hollywood types, up-close photographs and video only – before he took a break from filming to visit Daphne, Robert, and their two kids for the holidays. Cape Cod for Christmas was one of his personal favorite adventures. The Santa boat parade in Hyannis. The Holly Folly festivities in Provincetown. The extravagant gingerbread castles they made every year at the local inn… from the cookie strolls to the light competitions, he'd loved all of it since his own childhood. He made sure to clear out his busy schedule every year for the month of December to be home for everything-Christmas, especially while the kids were young and still believed in the magic of the season.

The more he thought about it, the more he felt like he couldn't wait to head home for the holidays. The hometown where he'd grown up, and now where his sister and her family still lived. He might not want a family of his own, but he spent every December with his sister and hers.

Grinning at the memories of hanging with his niece and nephew in years past, he punched in his code to get her voicemail, hoping she had called with gift ideas for his niece Karly. What was appropriate to give a three-year-old who was half princess and half ninja?

As he listened to the message, his smile slipped from his face.

Mike came to stand next to him at the railing. "Hey man, you're white as a sheet. Since when do you get seasick?" He noticed the cell phone in his hand. "Bad news?"

Zack stared at the phone. "The worst. I need to get home."

Shaking his head, Mike pulled out his own phone and brought up a calendar. "Sure. Next week we're filming in Kenya, but I can front-load that and you can be out of there and leaving for stateside by Saturday. The following Monday at the latest."

"You don't understand. My sister. There was an accident."

CHAPTER 1

October
Chatham, Massachusetts

"Thank you for coming." Zack stood last in line, shaking yet another hand, a headache forming behind his eyes. His black suit felt too tight on his shoulders, the necktie too tight around his throat. Nothing had felt comfortable for weeks now, but today was the worst yet.

"Your sister and her husband were such wonderful people." The older woman shook her head in sorrow, eyes downcast. Her grey hair was pulled into a tight bun, firmly shellacked into place.

Zack noticed how the overhead lights reflected off her bun the same way Mike's bald head reflected sunlight. Had it really been only a few weeks ago when they stood side by side in Kleinbaai Harbour watching the sunrise?

And now he was back in his hometown, two months earlier than planned.

For a totally different reason.

He pulled himself back to the moment. To the neighbor standing in front of him, voicing her condolences. He should remember her name. She looked vaguely familiar, but then, so did everyone in this small town. He and his sister had grown up here in Chatham. Daphne and Robert had stayed and put down roots of their own.

"Such a tragedy. And with the kids so young."

Zack could only nod in response, going through the motions on autopilot as the older woman shuffled out into the sunshine and another neighbor took her place to shake his hand and say the words.

"I'm sorry for your loss," the next neighbor started, and Zack tuned out.

He'd heard the same words repeated over and over in one form or another since he'd returned from South Africa. The trip back to the States felt like it took forever, pushing to get home as fast as possible with one delay after another. Everything still seemed to move in slow motion as the facts rolled around in his head on an endless doom loop.

Plane crash.

Daphne and Robert died instantly, they said.

Just like his parents.

The mirror to his own childhood tragedy made the entire thing sort of surreal. Except of course, the situation was very, very real. And so much worse.

When Zack's parents died, Daphne was already in college. Not in kindergarten, like Bobby. And Zack had just started high school. Not preschool, like Karly. It had been easy enough for Daphne to transfer to a college closer to home and be there for her younger brother. Keep the house they grew up in. Let him stay at the same high school until graduation.

Or at least, he'd always figured it was easy enough. He'd never asked her.

She came home for the funeral and never left, because that's what family did. Transferred her credits over from Yale and finished her degree at the local community college in Hyannis. Easy peasy.

Daphne made everything seem easy. Even when it wasn't.

It suddenly struck him how much of her own life Daphne gave up for him. Or put on hold. By the time Zack went off to college, she'd already met Robert, fallen in love, and decided to stay on Cape Cod to raise a family. She sold their childhood home, splitting the proceeds down the middle and putting Zack's share in a trust he couldn't touch until after he earned a degree. A smart move on her part, as he thought about dropping out at least once a semester. And after graduation, the money was there for him to start up his tour business with his newly minted business degree.

Now it was his turn to step up. Family should take care of family.

And those two little kids were now his responsibility. His family.

Their grandmother, however, held a different opinion on the matter.

Daphne's in-laws stood to his left, also shaking hands and accepting hugs and condolences from old friends and neighbors. Agnes and Richard Mills sold their Chatham home and retired to Florida several years ago, but still had plenty of connections on Cape. The memorial service had been standing room only, and the cynical part of his brain kept whispering that some of the mourners weren't here for his sister, but for the chance to meet a television star.

Several had even admitted it and asked for selfies in the receiving line. *Not cool.* He closed his eyes and drew in a long, slow breath, trying to ignore the growing ache behind his eyes.

"So sorry for your loss. I didn't know her well, but she seemed like a great person."

He grimaced before he could stop himself. *Great. Another funeral crasher.*

But when he opened his eyes, a blonde, blue-eyed ghost from his past, wearing a tight black dress and looking like his teenaged wet dreams come to life. "Erin? Erin Brannigan?"

A pretty pink flush colored her cheeks. "I didn't know whether you'd remember me."

"Yeah, well, our graduating class was pretty small." At forty-two students, theirs had been the last big class to graduate from Chatham High School, *big* obviously being a relative term.

Her blush deepened to crimson as he stood there silently drinking her in. Golden hair pulled back in a demure bun at the nape of a long neck graced by a simple silver chain. Funeral appropriate little black dress that showed off a hell of a lot more curves than he remembered from high school. Back then, Erin had been the girl in braids and baggy overalls. Said overalls being nearly always splattered with paint.

"You were going to be an artist," he suddenly remembered, speaking his thoughts out loud. "Determined to move to London or Paris and make a living with your paintings." His mind conjured a picture of a teenaged Erin, standing in front of their history class and delivering a fiery, impassioned speech on the importance of art in the world.

He'd been enraptured by her spark, by the fire he saw in her eyes, wondering why he'd spent the last four years without that kind of fire in his life. Without getting to know her better. But the timing was bad, since they both had big plans to leave Cape Cod after graduation, each dreaming of something bigger than their small hometown.

Didn't stop him from fantasizing about getting her out of those overalls.

The blonde in front of him now graced him with a wide smile, the kind that felt like the sun bursting through on a cloudy day and warming him from the inside out. "Good memory. And you either wanted to be a famous Hollywood star, or a stuntman. Seems like you've got the best of both worlds. I love your television show, by the way. I don't know how you talk those people into going on those crazy adventures all around the world."

"Thanks," he said, pride puffing out his chest just a little, basking in that incredible smile. "I don't talk anyone into an adventure, or not usually. They pay for the thrill-seeking privileges. And to have the opportunity to hang out with me."

She rolled those pretty blue eyes and laughed, just as he'd intended. Okay, maybe funeral crashers weren't the worst thing in the world.

"Humble as always, I see."

"And what about you? Lighting the art world on fire yet?"

The corners of her full pink lips turned down and her eyes shuttered, the slightest hitch in her voice as she replied, "Life doesn't always work out the way we imagine it will when we're kids."

He didn't know what to say to that. They stared at each other for long moments, Zack trying to come up with a witty retort but getting stuck on the fact that she looked so... perfect. Why was it again that he hadn't he struck up a friendship with her back in school? With only forty-two kids in their class, had there really been such strict boundaries between the jocks and the art nerds?

Maybe he could call her up to go for drinks or something later, catch up more. Hear about her fabulous bohemian life, wherever she'd ended up, since it sounded like Paris hadn't worked out the way she planned. He was about to ask when someone down the line cleared their throat loudly. Glancing over, he saw his Great Aunt Dolores standing next in the line, checking her watch none too subtly.

Erin started to shuffle forward, glancing over her shoulder as if noticing the people behind her for the first time. "Anyway, I don't want to hold up the line. Like I said, I didn't know your sister very well, but I wanted to see you."

Right. She came to meet the TV star. The warm feelings he'd had moments before fizzled away, the cold and cynical taking their place. "Well, mission accomplished."

She looked taken aback by his change of tone. "I'm sorry for your loss. If I can help in any way, please let me know." She thrust her hand out between them for him to shake, obviously ready to move along and get on with her actual life, just like everyone else who'd come this morning. Like the drivers who slow down to gawk at an accident before hurrying along, thankful it wasn't their car in flames.

The words were meant to sooth, to placate, and yet they triggered something dark inside him.

Because that's all they were.

Words.

Everyone had thrown out those same phrases when his parents died. Everyone said the words. Very few meant any of them.

The words didn't keep him and his sister from standing in line at the food pantry. Or losing their telephone when they couldn't pay all the bills and had to choose. Or having to wear the same tight jeans day after day, long after he'd grown out of them.

In the end, you could only count on family. And sometimes, not even then.

Any thoughts of how good his old classmate looked in that curve-hugging dress, or how easy it would be to pull the clips from her long golden hair and taste those pink lips... those thoughts faded away. He hadn't really known her back in high school, and he certainly didn't know her now.

"Thanks for coming," he told her, keeping a lid on the sudden anger bubbling in his gut, his tone as neutral as hers. "Maybe I'll see you around town."

Her polite mask faltered. She tipped her head to one side and smiled. "Yeah, I'm pretty sure you'll be seeing me on a regular basis. Almost every day, if you're lucky."

What the fuck? "That's pretty presumptuous."

She quirked a brow, still smiling that polite smile. "Excuse me?"

He leaned closer, his lips skimming her ear while he tried to ignore her intoxicating scent. *Lemons, ocean breezes, and something else.* Something he might want to explore in another time, another place. *But not here. Not now. Not with her.*

"You know how good you look," he whispered roughly, "poured into that tight little dress. But Erin. Let's be real." He felt the shiver run through her as he breathed her name into her ear. "I doubt anything between us would be an every-day thing. You're more of a long weekend. At best."

He pulled back enough to see her eyes widen in shock before filling with anger.

"Good to see the show producers don't have to fake your overin-flated ego," she whisper-yelled at him.

"Sweetheart, I think you got that twisted around." He smirked at her, but still kept his voice low enough for her ears only. "You're the one who propositioned me. In the receiving line at my sister's funeral, a woman you admit not knowing I might add."

"Zack…"

He waved away the excuse on her lips. "I know I'm famous and all, but have some self-respect and leave before this gets more awkward than it already is."

Angry energy rolled off her in waves. "I guess I'll see you around, Zack."

"Not if I see you first." Okay, it was childish. But damn. She got under his skin.

Great Aunt Dolores shuffled forward, her enormous black and grey caftan swirling around her like a slow-moving hurricane, her torrent of words buffeting against him as he watched Erin stomp out of the church. "Sorry to rush you along, but I promised Robert's mother I'd be at the house helping the caterer put out the buffet, and make sure the kids are doing okay with the neighbors. Which, by the way, I think the kids should've been allowed to come to the church but that Agnes… well, water under the bridge now. And of course I'm late because you know me, I got talking books with the reverend and now here I am at the back of the line with the rest of the stragglers. But I couldn't leave the church without one more hug."

She pulled Zack into a full body squeeze and spoke softly in his ear. "The irony of it all is not lost on me, kiddo. This has to be tugging at some painful memories."

Zack felt his throat tighten. He returned the squeeze and wished things had been different when his own parents died. Wished there'd been family members he could count on for help. But both his parents were only children. The only blood family left was Dolores. His grandfather's younger sister.

She lived an hour down the highway in Wellfleet, where she'd owned a bookstore and coffee shop for just about forever, catering to an endless stream of scruffy writers who spent summers on the Cape trying to write their next Great American Novel. She'd been there for Daphne and Zack intermittently during his childhood, usually at holidays and funerals, but even back then wasn't someone Zack thought of as "reliable." He was surprised to hear she'd volunteered to help with anything.

He cleared his throat, pushing away the emotions clawing for escape. "I guess I'll see you back at the house," he said diplomatically as he pulled away, not wanting to get into painful memories neither of them wanted to actually talk about.

"I'm glad to see you reconnected with Erin Brannigan."

"Reconnected?"

"You went to high school with the girl, if my old memory isn't failing me."

"Yeah, I went to school with her. Her dad was my history teacher."

"See? You remember her. Which is good, because she's going to be very important to you these next few months."

Zack couldn't help the disbelieving snort that escaped his mouth. "She certainly seemed to think so."

"With good reason," Aunt Dolores said primly. "She'll play a big part in your transition back to Chatham."

"And why's that?"

"She's Bobby's kindergarten teacher."

CHAPTER 2

"*A*rrogant. Annoying. *Asshole.*" Erin fumed as she started up her ancient Volvo and left the church parking lot. That last word wasn't really an adjective, and would cost her fifty cents into Hailey's swear jar, but it fit the man to a T. "Asshole," she repeated with conviction, upping her payment to a dollar. "Why would he think I was propositioning him?"

Thoughts of Zack Donovan's perfectly coiffed curls and smirking face filled her mind, his parting words dripping like venom in her ear. Okay, so her dress might be a little bit tight over her post-baby hips and boobs, but it was the only black dress in her closet. She'd thought herself lucky it still fit at all since she didn't have money to waste on a new one.

The minute she'd walked into the church and seen him standing at the front talking with the priest, it felt like the breath had been knocked from her body. Zack Donovan. Here. In Chatham. Looking better than any man has a right to, even better in person than he did on television. Better than any of her teenaged fantasies about him finally noticing her and asking her out.

She stood in line with the other mourners, not sure if he'd remember her at all from high school. But she'd enjoyed meeting

Daphne and Robert at Back-to-School night. She needed to let him know she would do her best as Bobby's teacher to keep an eye on him and support him through this terrible time, for as long as he and the kids stayed in Chatham. With Zack's globe-trotting lifestyle, who knows how long that would be.

For a moment there in the receiving line, she'd lost herself in those remarkable eyes of his, the ones she'd daydreamed about on and off since they first captured her attention in sixth grade. An everchanging moonstone color, depending on the weather or his mood or any of a number of factors.

Back in the day, she'd gone to the local hardware store and gathered all the grey paint swatches from the shelf to try to name the colors she saw swirling in his eyes. From "Pearl River" to "Pewter" to "Shark Fin" to "Charcoal Mist", and everything in between. Sometimes she'd try to match the color with her acrylics, but could never hit on any of those magical shifting tones.

She kept a running tally of the changing colors on the inside cover of her 3-ring binder… right up until his parents' accident, after which they'd just been a lifeless, "Classic Flat" grey for the rest of the school year. After a while she'd stopped keeping track. Life moved on.

She let out a frustrated growl and banged her fist against the steering wheel. She had no idea what set him off like that, but realized it probably had less to do with her than with the circumstances. To lose his sister the same way he lost his parents... Zack had every right to be angry with the world at large. She didn't begrudge him the anger. On some level, she understood that kind of anger. When the world doesn't live up to your expectations. Or when people don't live up to them.

And yet, she still envied him. She'd always wanted to travel the world. Have all the adventures. For those first years after high school, she had. Until she had to make a choice. And she chose to come back to Cape Cod.

By the time she'd pulled into the driveway, she'd let go of her annoyance with Zack. Okay, with ninety percent of the annoyance. At least seventy five percent. His nephew Bobby was a sweetheart of a kid, and deserved better than dealing with adults who couldn't get along.

"Mom, I'm home," Erin called as she kicked off her heels on the mat by the front door and wandered down the breezy hallway. *Mom must have all the windows open today,* she thought, wondering how much longer the nice weather would last. Autumn on Cape Cod was one of her favorite times of the year. Back to school, quieter streets without the summer tourists, warm weekends on near-empty beaches. *In fact, today's warm enough to be a beach day...*

"We're out on the deck, honey," her mother yelled back. "Come join us."

She grabbed a Honeycrisp apple from the basket on the counter as she passed through the kitchen and out the open French doors. She spotted them on the back lawn, heads bent together, her daughter's blonde curls ruffling in the breeze, her mother's straight blonde bob pulled back with a colorful headband, something she often did when the pair worked on crafts together. Erin's heart panged for a moment, wondering what kind of fun she'd missed out on.

"Hey you two. I ended up not going to the Donovan house for the reception, so I'm back earlier than planned. What have you all been up to all morning?"

Her daughter beamed at her, a creamy brown mask covering the entire lower half of her face. "Grandma taught me how to make pudding-in-a-bag! We threwed it around and everything, and it turned into pudding!" She held up her squished Ziplock bag, traces of the treat still coating the insides.

Her mother gave her an equally wide grin, albeit hers wasn't smeared with chocolate. "I thought we'd take advantage of this summer-like day and picnic in the yard. Yes, we each ate a PB and J first. And then dessert! Remember when we did this with your scout troop when you were young, Erin?"

"Sure do, Mom." She crunched into her apple, kind of wishing it was chocolate pudding instead and realizing it was those kinds of food choices that prompted Zack's comment about being *poured into* her dress, as if it were actually bursting at the seams and not just a little – or a lot – tight. Her next thought was to dismiss that nonsense out of her head. Yes, her body had changed since the last time she saw him, but that was life. Things change. Zack didn't look the same as he did back in high school either.

No, he looks even better, the traitorous voice in her head whispered. Each episode of his show made certain to include a scene where Zack was taking his shirt off for one reason or another. Any (and possibly every) female viewer of *Epic Adventures* knew the man worked out religiously and had the broad shoulders and six-pack abs to prove it. And that tribal tattoo of a stylized shark on his left shoulder, the one she wanted to lick. The one that probably tasted better than chocolate pudding…

She cleared her throat, trying to clear her thoughts at the same time. "What do you say about heading to the beach for the afternoon? It might be the last good beach day for a while."

"Considering it's already mid-October, that's an excellent proba- bility." Her mother stood, then helped Hailey to her feet. "Come along, munchkin. Let's get you changed into your swimsuit."

They started into the house before the words registered with Erin. "Hailey doesn't need her bathing suit, Mom. I'm sure the ocean is too cold for that, even if the sun is shining strong."

Her mother merely laughed and kept ushering her grandchild toward her room. "She's six, Erin. She'll be in and out of the water more times than you'll be able to count and won't notice the cold until it's dark out. And maybe not even then. You were always the same way, living for the moment."

"Not anymore," Erin grumbled under her breath. Nowadays she was more of a rule follower and risk avoider. She'd been reckless and *lived for the moment*, and look where that got her. Thirty-three and living with her parents. With her father-less child. *Well, there was tech- nically a father*, she thought bitterly. *He just prefers his happy-go-lucky bachelor life in London, rather than taking a more active role in his daugh- ter's world.*

The world she'd made for herself and Hailey when she'd left London, pregnant and broken-hearted. Maureen and Tom Brannigan let her move back home, Erin and her human-to-be, welcoming her with open arms and without too many awkward questions. She moved back into her old room, and Maureen's sewing room became a nursery. After Hailey's birth, both parents supported Erin's decision to get her teaching degree at the local community college.

And here they were. Almost seven years later, with Hailey now attending the same school where Erin worked. Living with the proud grandparents, who insisted they were thrilled to have them there… as long as babysitting wasn't taken for granted.

She picked up her black heels and headed for the stairs to change her own clothes. *No bathing suit for me*, Erin thought with a shiver. But her little black dress was certainly not beach appropriate.

"C'mon, Mom." Hailey appeared at the top of the staircase, barefoot and dressed in her Cookie Monster themed bathing suit, smile wide and bright without the chocolate halo. "Grandma said she'd grab buckets and shovels from the shed and meet us at the car."

"Okay, okay, you're going to wait a minute. I can't go to the beach wearing this," Erin said with a laugh.

Hailey frowned, looking her up and down as if to find the problem. "Why not? You look pretty."

"Thanks, sweetie." Her heart warmed at the simple logic of a six-year-old. "I think I might have trouble walking in the sand with these heels. And I know I'll be more comfortable in shorts and t-shirt when we build our sandcastle."

The look of deep thought on her daughter's face made her heart twist, in a good way. *God, I love this kid. Leo doesn't know what he's missing out on.*

Her ex might think he was living the dream with his ever-changing parade of girlfriends, but he'd missed the first six years of his daughter's life. And Erin was pretty darn sure he planned to miss the next six. And the six after that. Forever. Sending a birthday card and check once a year wasn't the same thing as being a dad.

She ruffled the blonde curls on top of her daughter's head. "Let's make it a race, yeah? I'll bet I can change my clothes faster than you can find your blue hat and flip flops to go with that swimsuit."

Hailey's eyes lit up with the challenge. "On your mark, get set, go!" The kid was off like a racehorse, sprinting back down the hallway to her room.

TWO HOURS and one giant sandcastle later, Erin flopped into a beach chair next to her mother, tired but happy. The two of them watched in contented silence as Hailey decorated every inch of their sand sculpture with the small pebbles and shells they'd gathered on their walk along the shoreline. Gulls wheeled overhead making lazy circles over the calm ocean, gentle waves rolling up on the beach in a constant, soothing rhythm.

"She's a good girl," her mother pronounced, breaking the silence. She opened the small cooler and handed Erin a can of her daughter's favorite brand of lemonade.

"Yup," Erin agreed with a smile, popping the top and letting the cool, citrusy goodness ease her parched throat.

"You've done a great job with her, given the circumstances. Being a single mom isn't easy."

Erin's smile faded at the sudden turn of conversation. Over the years, the subject of Hailey's father had come up a few times. Her parents were fairly traditional and big believers in the sanctity of family. She lowered the drink and looked at her mother, who was still seemingly absorbed by watching Hailey play. "Is there something you want to say, Mom?"

"Just that a child should get the chance to know and love both parents."

"We've been over this ground before, Mom. Leo Kensington made his choices. He broke up with me when he found out I was pregnant. Sent me packing from both our flat and the art studio. I didn't run away, he pushed me. Hard. And he didn't waste any time replacing me, if the tabloids have it right."

"People can change their minds, Erin."

"Yeah right."

If Leo had wanted to change his mind, he'd had plenty of time to get in touch. He knew where she and Hailey lived, as evidenced by the checks that arrived like clockwork every year on the tenth of December, five days before Hailey's actual birthday. She took another sip of the drink, hoping to wash away the bitterness she always felt when she thought of her ex.

"He called the house today, while you were at that memorial service."

An icy chill shot through her body, lemonade flying from her mouth in a wide spray across the sand. "What? Why? Did you talk with him?"

Her mother looked bemused by the question. "Yes. I answered the phone. That's how I know it was him."

Erin wiped the drips of lemonade from her chin. "Does Hailey know? Did she talk to him?"

The amusement turned into a frown. "Erin Leigh Brannigan. You know me better than that."

"Sorry, I'm sorry. What did he want?"

"He wants to meet Hailey."

"No." The answer was easy. No. He'd given up that right years ago.

When she'd first met him, Erin thought he looked like a young Colin Firth, straight from the set of *Pride and Prejudice,* with the dark curls and wide shoulders and narrow hips... Unfortunately, she found out the hard way that behind his good looks and posh British accent, the man was a cheating snake. The thought of flying across the Atlantic with her daughter because the spineless asshole was finally ready to see her face-to-face sent waves of unhappy rumbles rolling through her belly.

But... a kneejerk reaction that wasn't fair to Hailey either. If Leo really wanted to meet his daughter, maybe Erin should be the bigger person about it, if only for her daughter's sake. If she could control the situation, temper her daughter's expectations, maybe neither of them would end up getting hurt by the careless man who threw them both away in the first place.

Now that she started thinking about it, she saw the logic in letting the two meet. Hailey asked about her father the year before, when she realized the other kids in preschool each had two parents and she only had one. Meeting Leo might help answer those questions Erin knew lurked unspoken in her daughter's head. Maybe they could plan a trip to London over the next summer vacation. She'd have a few months between now and June to prepare her daughter, make sure she understood the situation, or at least as much as a young child could. Because she knew she shouldn't expect much of anything from Leo. It's not like he'd ever even called before, not to check on her or his daughter.

But… Hailey was his child. Biologically, at least.

She metaphorically pulled on her big girl panties and tried to think logically about next steps. If she started looking for cheap flights and hotels now, she could probably afford it. Leo's annual checks were tucked safely into a savings account for Hailey's college fund. There was no way she'd touch that for anything else, not even a trip to introduce the two. Just because the rich jerk sent money for the last six years didn't mean he always would, and Erin planned to squirrel away as much as she could for her daughter's future.

She blew out a long, slow breath, realizing her mother hadn't said another word to argue for or against. "You're right. Hailey has every right to meet her father but I don't want to see her disappointed. Maybe… I'll take a look at travel arrangements tonight, after she's in bed. I don't want to tell her any of this until it's a done deal. We can visit London next summer after school gets out."

"Next summer? That seems pretty far away." Maureen's frown made Erin squirm.

"Well, I need time to plan, and to prepare Hailey. She hasn't asked me too much about… her father. All she knows is that he lives on the other side of that ocean right there." Erin jabbed a finger toward the waves lapping at the sand. "She's never asked why."

"She will eventually."

Erin sighed. "Yeah, I know. Okay. Maybe we can travel over April vacation, if the fares are cheap enough. Does that sound better to you? That's a short six months away."

"What about Christmas vacation?"

Something in her mother's tone made Erin's skin prickle, but her rejection of the idea poured out in a fast stream, like the water now pouring from Hailey's bucket.

"Leave you and Dad alone for Christmas? Miss any of Hailey's favorite holiday traditions? No. Not going to happen. Besides, that's too soon, and airfares over the holidays are always outrageous. No. Definitely not."

Her mother stared at her unblinking.

Erin lifted her lemonade as if to toast her mother. "If Leo wants to meet her so badly, he can be the one to travel. He's got plenty of money, the smarmy bastard. He should come here to see her."

Maureen nodded. "That's exactly what I thought, too. He's rich. He should pay for the airfare. Which is why I invited him to spend Christmas with us."

For the second time in the course of the conversation, lemonade spewed out across the sand in front of Erin. Eyes wide, she stared at her mother. "You can't be serious."

Her mother nodded again, blue eyes completely unfazed. "Of course I'm serious. Because you're right. He's got the money. And he's an adult. If he wants to know his daughter, he should be the one to come here and meet that little girl on her own ground."

Which made sense, now that Erin thought about it. But it didn't stop the anger from churning her gut and bubbling out. "You had no right to invite him! How could you do that to me? To us?"

And Christmas? Too soon! Halloween was mere weeks from now, with meant Thanksgiving in a month, and Christmas practically right on its heels. Two months to prepare Hailey to meet a man she knew absolutely nothing about?

Only two short months to get *herself* mentally prepared to see Leo again?

Her mother looked contrite as she laid a gentle hand on Erin's knee. "It's been years, sweetie. Already too long to wait for this introduction, if you ask me."

"I didn't ask you. And you didn't ask me either. Why didn't we talk about this first, before you go and invite him for Christmas? Who does that, Mom?"

"Honey, I'm sorry. When he called, he sounded sad. He said he was sorry he never met your father and I, and said he really wanted to meet Hailey, to see you again, as soon as possible. I told him it was ridiculous to expect you to fly to England."

Erin snorted. "Damn straight."

"I never actually expected him to accept my invitation."

Which placated Erin a bit, the idea her mother had thrown the invitation as a challenge and not as part of some misguided attempt to reconcile her daughter and her ex. But it still left so many open questions.

And it still meant Leo was coming to the Cape for Christmas.

"Why now, all of a sudden like this? What changed?"

Her mother shook her head. "I don't know. He didn't say. But he's coming to the US in December."

"But why?"

When Erin first told Leo about the pregnancy, he'd raged around their Notting Hill studio, overturning furniture and smashing dishes. He made it crystal clear that he never wanted to be a father or have a family, and told her in no uncertain terms that if she wanted to go through with having the baby, she'd be on her own. He wanted no part.

She always assumed it was someone else in his family that guilted Leo into sending the birthday money to Hailey, the cards unsigned and the check cut by the family's solicitor. She'd met his parents once or twice at charity events in London, stereotypical British aristocrats, with upper lips so stiff they might've been cast from cement. She could see one of them telling him it was his *familial duty*.

But Hailey was a Brannigan. Not a Kensington.

"Why is he coming?" she asked again, when her mother didn't answer.

"You can ask him when you call him back."

"Call him back? Why?" Erin felt like a broken record, but none of this made sense.

"He wants to talk with you, obviously. Probably to plan the details of the trip," her mother said. "Erin, your father and I love you, and we love being Hailey's grandparents. But if there's a chance to make things right between you and Leo, don't you owe it to that little girl?"

"I don't owe Leo anything. He made his choice. I made mine."

"Agreed. But what about you? I'm sure living with your parents is not how you envision the rest of your life. You've been home for seven years now. Isn't it time for your next adventure?"

Those thoughts she'd had earlier at the church circled in her head. Her high school fantasies of traveling the globe, experiencing new cultures, visiting exotic settings. She'd stopped dreaming of adventure once Hailey came into her life, choosing to move back home, safe and secure in her small town. The only traveling she did these days was through books and TV shows like Zack's.

"Are you kicking us out?"

"Never." Maureen leaned over and patted Erin's knee. "You will always have a home with us. If you need it. But you're still young, sweetie. I'm just saying you need to think about what you want out of life."

"And you think it might be Leo?"

"He left a number where you can reach him in Surrey."

"Surrey? He moved out of London?" Erin remembered that Leo's parents lived in the countryside. Some sort of manor or something in some sleepy village that Leo professed to despise.

"I have it all written down back at the house," her mother said with a wave of a hand as if the conversation was complete.

"Mom, you know that this is far from over. You can't make decisions like this for me and my daughter."

"I'm not making decisions for you," Maureen sighed. "I'm trying to help you see that you have choices you need to make. You can't hide from him forever."

"I was never hiding in the first place," Erin grumbled, looking away.

"Have you finished Hailey's Halloween costume? She was asking me earlier."

The abrupt change in conversation gave Erin whiplash. "Umm, almost. I finished painting the family crest on the felt for her cape, I just need to attach it to her armor." The conversation continued along the safer path of discussing Halloween plans at the elementary school, and the party at the Community Center on Halloween night that the whole family planned to attend instead of trick-or-treating door to door – a tough thing to do in a town where the majority of homes belonged to summer-only residents.

When her daughter decided she wanted to dress up as a knight instead of a princess, Erin hadn't argued. The only thing she'd drawn the line at was including a sword as part of the costume, but they'd come to a compromise of sorts and bought a large stuffed dragon, with purple scales and golden wings, for Hailey to carry around. If she couldn't slay dragons with a sword, she was going to train them instead.

Why not? Why couldn't her little girl be anything she wanted to be in life?

Her mother's words echoed in her head. *Isn't it time for your next adventure?*

She ignored those prodding words to focus on what Hailey wanted. It didn't matter that her own hopes and dreams hadn't turned out the way Erin originally planned. Her daughter was her world now. She wouldn't change that for anything. Oh, she was still angry with Maureen for the underhanded way she'd orchestrated Leo's visit, no doubt about that. But maybe her mom was also a little bit right.

Seven years was a long time, and Hailey needed to meet her father.

Even if it meant Erin had to face seeing Leo again.

But Leo was *definitely not* the next adventure on Erin's bucket list.

She just wasn't sure what was.

CHAPTER 3

$\mathcal{T}$he last of the guests and mourners finally left as the light began to fade from the sky, leaving the house feeling even emptier than it had the night before the funeral. Zack leaned against the front door and blew out a heavy sigh. Just him and the kids now.

"Zack? Zack? Where'd you run off to?"

And Daphne's in-laws, he amended. *For however long they plan to stay.*

In the past, Robert's parents always seemed great when Zack's visits overlapped with theirs. They sold their Cape home and retired to Florida years ago, but returned to Chatham for a month or two each summer, staying with Daphne and Robert in the guest suite Robert added on to the back of the house. Not an in-law apartment, as it didn't have its own kitchen, but a large bedroom, sitting room and bathroom which let the couple have as much privacy during their visits as they wanted.

After being in the house with them for only a week, Zack had no idea how his sister ever put up with them for an entire month or more without going crazy. Or committing homicide. Or both.

Then again, Daphne had put up with his all of his teen angst and raging hormones without batting an eyelash. No doubt about it, his sister was a saint.

Had been a saint. Past tense. He kept forgetting she and Robert were gone.

And now Robert's parents were Zack's problem.

Agnes Mills had an opinion about everything – none of them based in any kind of reality – which she happily shared often and loudly whether you wanted her advice or not. Richard Mills spent most of his time glued to the television in their guest rooms, watching sports and the sports news channels, barely coming out to join them for meals. Granted, the New England Patriots were doing well this season, but there were only so many football games to watch in a week. At least the man had been present for the funeral and the reception, even if he'd insisted on tuning the television in the family room to college football all afternoon.

She walked into the hall, still wearing the severe black dress and chunky pearl choker from the funeral. Sensible black shoes and one of Daphne's colorful aprons now accompanied the dress, but did nothing to soften the look. Bobby had whispered to him earlier that his grandmother looked like a witch, her hair dyed as black as her dress. Privately, Zack had to agree with his nephew.

"There you are, Zack. Now, what should we do with the leftover food? The kids shouldn't eat all of those cold cuts, they say all those nitrates aren't good for little tummies. I told your aunt not to order so many but she didn't listen to me. Should we call the food pantry and see if we can donate the rest? And all the casseroles people brought, I'm wondering if we should keep those or throw it all away since we have no idea what ingredients they used. This one probably has gravy from a can." She was holding a glass casserole dish, frowning at the contents as if they might be poisoned.

Canned gravy was the least of Zack's problems at the moment.

"Daphne's neighbor Alison brought the shepherd's pie that you're holding. I'm sure it's fine," he told her. "The kids love that stuff, and they love ham and cheese sandwiches too." He followed her back into the dining room, where half-empty platters and dishes covered the table. There really wasn't a whole lot of food left that he could see.

"Agnes, there's not enough here to bring to the local pantry, besides the fact that I don't think they take prepared foods like this."

Her frown deepened as she dropped the casserole back on the table with a thud. "Well, that's ridiculous. If people are sitting there at the pantry hungry and looking for food, they should take whatever they can get. Do they think they're too good for our leftovers? This is the problem with people today. They all think they're entitled to something more."

Zack closed his eyes and counted to ten, a technique he'd developed years ago when dealing with whiny – albeit paying – customers on his tours. A technique he'd been using a lot in the past two weeks when dealing with Agnes. He'd figured out early on that there was no use arguing or trying to introduce little things like logic, or facts, into the conversation. No sense pointing out to her that the local food pantry didn't have customers sitting at tables waiting to be fed like at a restaurant. It's not how the system worked. He should know, having visited weekly through his teens, after his own parents died.

Opening his eyes again, he picked up the casserole dish she'd abandoned and walked into the kitchen. Grabbing the aluminum foil, he covered the dish and found a spot for it in the already crowded refrigerator. Maybe Agnes had a small point about there being too much food in the house for the five of them. Six if you counted Great Aunt Dolores, but Zack wasn't sure if she planned to stay in town for a few days or if she'd already headed back to Wellfleet. Speaking of heading home…

"Agnes, how long are you and Richard planning to stay in town?"

She entered the kitchen with the platter of deli meat and a surprised look on her face. "What do you mean? Are you trying to get rid of us?"

"No, that's not what I meant," he said, taking the serving tray from her hands and putting it on the counter. He pulled the plastic wrap out of the drawer to wrap the rest of the ham and cheese. "But I know you had to postpone that cruise when you got the terrible news, so that you could stay here longer with Bobby and Karly." The original plan had been for the grandparents to stay with the kids for two weeks while Daphne and Robert went away for a week-long getaway to Mexico. That went out the window when the sightseeing plane crashed in the jungle. It took weeks to bring the bodies back to the states for the funeral.

Agnes smoothed a hand down her black skirt, not meeting his eyes. "Of course we stayed! Canceled the cruise completely! They're our grandbabies and they needed us to be here. And where were you? On the other side of the world. Swimming with sharks, no less!"

The last part sounded like an accusation, making Zack bristle. "I was working. My job takes me all over the world, as both a travel guide and a television host. You *know* that, Agnes."

"Yes, your so-called job takes you to lots of dangerous and unsavory spots," she agreed. "And what do you plan to do with your niece and nephew while you're galivanting around the globe, jumping off cliffs and swimming with sharks? Are you planning to teach Bobby how to wrestle alligators before he hits middle school?"

"I'm going to take care of them," Zack insisted, keeping his voice calm. "Just like Daphne took care of me when our parents died."

"Don't be ridiculous," Agnes scoffed. "You're not fit to be their guardian, Zachary Donovan. My son always said you're nothing but a thrill seeker who can't stay in one place for long. Always chasing the next new adventure. Those kids deserve better. They need a stable home and community."

"This is a stable home and community," he argued, ignoring the stab of pain brought on by her callous words. Words she wielded like knives, cutting him to the bone, even if he knew they weren't true. If Robert didn't think he was *stable*, he wouldn't have named him guardian to his kids.

Although, the guy probably never thought his plane would go down either.

"Daph and I grew up in this town. She wants, wanted, the same kind of childhood for her kids. She and Robert both wanted that. They told me as much last Christmas when I was home for the holidays."

She ignored what he said about her son's wishes, waving it away like a bad smell. "You should sign the paperwork and hand over custody to me. Richard and I will take them back to Florida and everything will be as it should be."

"We've been through this argument enough times already. Daphne and Robert chose me as guardian. They want the kids to stay here on Cape Cod."

"Which is ridiculous too. There is nothing wrong with our place in Florida."

"You live in a retirement community, Agnes. Your two-bedroom townhouse has no backyard. They would be the only kids in the entire neighborhood. There aren't any elementary schools within a thirty minute radius. You like to go on long cruises three or four times a year. You and Richard travel almost as much as I do."

"But those kids are my family," she protested, her eyes glistening now.

"They're my family too," Zack countered, trying not to raise his voice, trying to stay calm. He knew this was hard for everyone, but he needed to honor his sister's last request. He owed it to her.

He blew out a long breath before continuing. "I don't want to fight with you, Agnes. You're their grandmother. There's no reason for us to argue. We should work together for their sakes, not against one another. I'm not going to keep them from you, but I am going to keep them here. With me."

She sniffed and flicked a finger underneath each eye to swipe away the moisture. "Well. I guess Daphne and Robert had their reasons when they wrote out their will, and made you the guardian for those two little innocent children. We'll have to wait and see how you grow into your new role, replacing my son as their father. Letting them forget all about their beautiful parents."

Zack raised both hands in a gesture of surrender. "Whoa now, is that what all this is about? Daphne and Robert haven't been gone a whole month yet, the pain is still sharp for all of us... and you're already worried about their memories fading away?"

She glared at him stubbornly, not agreeing or disagreeing with his assessment.

Zack shook his head and swore under his breath. "Agnes, I know I'm not their father. I'm not trying to replace Robert in their lives, not ever. And I think Daphne and your son knew that."

Agnes sniffed, her expression unconvinced, her eyes wet with unshed tears.

"I'm Uncle Zack, just like I've always been. And I plan to be there for Bobby and Karly."

"Well, we'll have to wait and see how it goes between now and Christmas." Agnes turned on her heel to leave the room.

"Christmas? What do you mean?"

She stopped and turned to face him again. "You think you can do this on your own? Take care of those two little angels all by yourself? Fine. Richard and I will leave at the end of the month. Leave you to figure it out for yourself. When we come back for the holidays, if things aren't all happy and settled by then... well, we'll have to reassess the situation."

"Reassess?"

"Make some decisions about what's truly best for Bobby and Karly. Which will most likely be moving to Florida to be with us." Agnes turned again and retreated from the kitchen, marching through the dining room and toward the guest room.

Hands on his hips, Zack closed his eyes and bowed his head, swearing softly. As if the situation wasn't hard enough, the woman had to put a deadline to it all.

The sound of sniffling caught his attention, and he opened his eyes to look around the kitchen. He was alone, but he definitely wasn't the one crying. Bending down, he checked underneath the kitchen table. A huddled lump of brown curls and neon pajamas had arms wrapped around one of the table legs. "Bobby? How long have you been under there?"

"Is Grandma going to make us go with her to Florida?" He sounded even younger than his six years, his voice small, his brown eyes wide and filled with tears. "I don't want to move, Uncle Z. Their house smells funny and there aren't any other kids around to play with. I like our house. I want to stay here."

Zack sat on the scuffed wood floor and scooted closer to where his nephew sat clinging to one of the thick pine table legs. Bright neon rocket ships zoomed in every direction across the flannel pants and shirt, the cheerful colors in contrast to the stark misery on Bobby's face.

Zack patted the boy's knee. "No one is going anywhere, little buddy. We're going to stay right here. You and me and Karly are going to live in this house all together. Does that sound okay?"

The boy sniffled again. "Not Florida?"

"Not Florida," Zack affirmed.

"Okay." He sniffled again. "But what about the stuff Grandma said about your job? And what about your TV show?"

"You and Karly are more important to me than the show," Zack told him. He was surprised to realize he really meant it. "You're my family. Family sticks together."

"Really?"

Zack moved closer and put an arm around Bobby's shoulders. "Did I ever tell you that I was there the day you were born?"

Bobby shook his head, his eye going wide. "You were?"

"Sure was," he said, nodding solemnly. "Now, I was there when Karly was born too, and maybe you remember that time because you and I were out in the waiting room together playing with your dinosaurs, but you, Bobby… you were the first brand new baby I ever saw in my whole life. And you know what my very first thought was when I saw you?"

The boy stared at him with rapt attention. "What?"

"I thought, wow. This little guy is part of my family now. He's going to be part of my world forever."

Bobby scrunched his forehead. "Forever?"

Zack nodded. "Forever. And right from that first time I held you in my arms, I knew I'd do anything for you. And then when Karly was born, same thing. You two are the most important things to me."

Bobby finally let go of the table leg and threw his arms around Zack. "I love you, Uncle Z."

"Me too, buddy." Zack squeezed him tight. "Me too."

CHAPTER 4

Halloween

"*D*on't go too far ahead," Erin called from where she stood on the sidewalk with a group of friends, fellow teachers at the elementary and middle schools, as her daughter dashed down the brick walkway that led to the Community Center's front entrance. She winced as Hailey dodged passed a family with a double stroller, nearly knocking it over. "I don't want to lose you in the crowd."

"Don't worry, Mom. I'm going to find Grandma and Gramps. You can meet me there," Hailey yelled back over her shoulder, with the confidence of a little girl who'd grown up in a small town, convinced she knew everything and everyone. Even if she was only six. Or six-and-three-quarters if you asked her about it.

Erin shook her head, smiling despite the small niggle of worry in the back of her mind. Her daughter knew her way around the building, knew all the teachers who were handing out candy, and knew the

Community Center workers all by name. How much trouble could she really get into?

Erin was the one who'd insisted on driving over alone with Hailey, instead of coming with her parents. She could admit she was avoiding her mother as much as possible, still angry with her about the Leo situation.

And by situation, she meant the fact that her mother had invited her ex to spend Christmas on Cape Cod with the family. *Without asking me first. Who does that?*

She tried to tune back into the conversation going on around her, discussing plans for the upcoming PTA holiday bazaar, a mere five weeks away. *And how did that happen?* she wondered. *December will be here before we know it.*

Which meant she really needed to talk to Leo soon about his visit. Or rather, see if he actually planned to travel to the US at all. Maybe meeting his daughter had been a drunken whim that he dismissed as soon as he sobered.

She wasn't sure which to hope for – that Leo was coming for the holidays, or that he'd decided it wasn't worth the effort. Either way, she needed to call and find out. And tell Hailey more about her father.

"Erin? Are you listening? I asked if you're going to put those artistic talents of yours to good use and be in charge of the face-painting booth this year." Her friend Claire MacDonald, one of the middle school teachers, was staring at her, waiting for an answer.

"What? Oh, right, face paint. Yes, of course I'll sign up for that."

"Is everything all right, Erin? You seem a little distracted."

Erin waved her hand back and forth in front of her face, as if to sweep away her errant thoughts. "I'm fine, really. A lot on my mind this past week."

Samantha Jones, another elementary school teacher in her friend circle, elbowed her in the ribs. "A lot on your mind, eh? Anything to do with the infamous Zack Donovan coming back to town?"

"Of course not. What are you talking about?"

Sam smirked. "I heard you and he might've had a heated exchange at his sister's funeral. I know his nephew is in your classroom, but I'd forgotten you two were in the same graduating class at Chatham High. Something left unresolved from way back when?"

"As if," Erin said with a snort of laughter. "He was a jock and I was an art nerd. End of story. At least as far as high school cliques were concerned. And let me tell you, that man is as much of an egotistical jerk as he was back then. He accused me of trying to hit on him at the funeral! Can you imagine?"

"If he looks half as good in person as he does on television, then yeah, I can totally believe women were hitting on him," Claire chimed in. "In line at the funeral, the grocery store, the bank… heck, anywhere a line forms!"

"Claire! You and Ed just got married this past summer!" From the heat pouring off her face, Erin knew she was blushing furiously. She was not about to admit she'd crushed on the guy back in the day, nor was she going to admit how truly delicious he looked in person.

Claire just laughed. "I'm married, not dead. And there's a reason they find any excuse to make him take his shirt off at least once every episode of *Epic Adventures*. Even when they were snowboarding in the Alps and all bundled in winter gear, they managed to have a shirtless hot tub scene after their day on the slopes. I think everyone and their mother wanted to lick that sexy shark tattoo on his shoulder."

"Well, I didn't proposition him in the receiving line, no matter what you might have heard," she told her friends. "I was trying to let him know I'm Bobby's kindergarten teacher, and he… he misunderstood what I said and decided to insult me. Something to the effect that I'm more of a *long weekend* than a long-term commitment."

Since these were her friends, they knew the story of how Leo kicked her to the curb as soon as she became pregnant. They jumped to her defense immediately.

"That bastard!" Claire's eyes flashed with anger. She'd been through her own bitter divorce back in Connecticut, before moving to Chatham and finding love again.

"Well, fudge," said Sam, throwing an arm around Erin's shoulders and giving her a quick squeeze. "I'm never gonna be able to watch that stupid show again."

"Have you seen him since the funeral?"

Erin shook her head. "Bobby was finally back in the classroom this week, but his grandmother has been doing the pickups from school. Small blessings, I guess. And probably a good thing for those kids, that their grandparents are here in town."

Sam frowned. "Didn't the Mills live over on Tipcart Lane? They sold that house a while back and moved to Florida. My friend Eliza was their realtor for the sale."

Emily O'Toole cleared her throat. "You know that my husband was good friends with Robert, Bobby's dad, right?"

Erin wondered where her friend was going with this. "Yes, and...?"

Her friend shrugged. "Robert thought the world of Zack, talked about how proud he and Daphne were of him, his business, the show... of all the guy accomplished after such a rocky childhood."

"Rocky childhood?" Erin snorted. "You forget I went to high school with him. He was an arrogant, self-absorbed meathead jock back then too."

Emily continued as if Erin hadn't spoken. "Daphne gave up a lot to come back to the Cape and raise him. Things were especially tough for both of them after the insurance money ran out. And then to lose his sister the same way they lost their parents... Zack probably wasn't acting like his best self when you saw him at the funeral."

Erin sighed, shaking her head again. She'd told herself the same thing after the funeral, hadn't she? "I get that, I do, but..."

Sam wrapped her in a hug. "Listen to Emily. Don't judge him on one bad interaction. And you certainly can't hold it against his nephew."

Erin drew back from her friend, eyes wide. "I would never hold anything against that little boy. He's a total sweetheart." *Unlike his uncle*, she added in her head. Even if Zack was all kinds of sexy, "sweet" was not a word she'd associate with the man.

"Now come on," Claire said, grabbing her hand. "We should get inside and find our kids. I'm hoping Ed and Kayleigh finish up trick-or-treating soon and are ready to head home. I had my fill of sugared-up middle schoolers yesterday!"

"Me too, although I think Hailey and I are here for the long haul. I promised to help my parents clean up their area after the event is over."

Claire laughed. "Better you than me, chickadee!"

They shared a commiserating laugh before heading down the well-worn brick path.

The Chatham Community Center had once been home to an elementary school, but the 1950s brick building had been repurposed and rehabbed into a variety of community all-purpose spaces to accommodate groups of every size, from scout troop meetings to yoga lessons to family karate classes and women's self-defense training. After-school programs for teens ranged from homework help to craft classes. The old school gym was brought up to more current standards, and played host to many organized sports including pickleball tournaments for adults every Sunday. For Halloween, the entire building had been transformed for a community-wide party, catering to every age group.

Erin stepped across the threshold and marveled at the cacophony echoing through the building. Overhead lights had been covered with orange cellophane, adding an eerie glow to the decorated halls. Erin knew from past years that each area of the Center had different themes for different age groups, some scarier than others, but nothing too nightmare-inducing. After all, the target age group here was twelve and under, although everyone was always welcome.

A signpost near the entrance pointed to the right for "Magical Fairyland," straight ahead toward the staircase for "Dancing Spiders and Skeletons," and to the left for "Vampires and Zombieland." Her father had left the house earlier dressed as a vampire, so Erin turned left to see if her daughter was braving it out on her own in the scariest section of the building.

Of course she is, Erin thought with a smirk. The kid had her knight costume on with her dragon tucked under one arm, and told her on the car ride over that she planned to trick-or-treat at every room in the Community Center no matter how scary.

"Because I know Gramps isn't a real *vampire, and Grandma wouldn't let*

anything blood-curdling or spine-chilling interfere with the fun. So I'm not afraid," she'd said with conviction. Erin figured her mother had used those phrases with Hailey – what did a six-year-old know about blood-curdling fears or spine-chilling screams – and was once again grateful that her daughter had such an overabundance of confidence.

As she rounded the corner, the smile faded from her face. Up ahead in the hallway, a group of gangly middle schoolers dressed as vampires, devils, and assorted ghouls circled around two smaller children. While spiderwebs of yarn dangled from the ceiling above and older children called encouragements from the sidelines, the two younger children rolled on the floor, aggressively tangled together and slapping at each other. Both dressed as knights in silver plastic armor and brightly decorated capes, wrestling on the ground and yelling loudly, their voices carrying above the rest of the noise.

"Give it back, you rotten excuse for a knight," screamed a high-pitched voice that sounded suspiciously like her daughter.

"Knights are supposed to fight dragons, not cuddle them like babies," the other knight yelled back, his voice also sounding familiar.

"Jerk face," yelled Hailey, tugging on the purple dragon and kicking at the boy's shins.

"Big baby," the boy sneered back at her, holding tight to his stolen prize and rolling over, dragging Hailey with him as he turned.

Erin pushed through the line of older kids and reached down to grab both children, pulling them apart and to their feet. Both costumes were dirty, hair a disheveled mess, plastic helmets tossed and forgotten.

Using her sternest teacher voice, she invoked their full names. "Bobby Donovan Mills! Hailey Kaye Brannigan! Stop fighting. Right. This. Instant!"

"He started it, Mom. He tried to steal Draco from me!"

"Girls can't be knights, you stupid-head. Only boys can be knights," said Bobby, crossing his arms over his plastic chest plate, his tone defiant, his brown curls a wild mess.

"Says who?" Hailey shot back at him, taking a step closer and yanking hard on the boy's cape. Instead of being sewn to his shoulders, the cape tied around his neck with a thick rope. When she tugged, Bobby let out a strangled sound. Draco fell to the ground as both hands flew to his throat to pull at the tightening cord.

"Hailey, stop that!" Erin let go of Bobby to grab both of her daughter's arms, turning her to look her in the eyes. "You could really hurt him like that."

"But Mom…" Angry tears filled Hailey's blue eyes, her chin still tipped up defiantly. "He's being mean."

"Still not a good reason to hurt him," Erin said, focusing only on her daughter and using a far quieter voice. Her daughter should know better than to fight, even if she hadn't started it. "Use your words to argue, not your hands."

Hailey closed her eyes and nodded in agreement. The middle schoolers who'd crowded around to egg on the fight melted away, leaving just the three of them standing in the middle of the hallway.

Erin blew out a long breath, trying to calm herself. It was a narrow tightrope to walk as a mother, between wanting your child to stand up for themselves and not wanting them to descend into violence. Any kind of violence. Even if it was hair pulling and name calling between kindergarteners.

She turned her steely gaze on Bobby, who stood quietly where she left him. She winced at the bright red welt around his neck, caused by her daughter. He'd already retrieved the stuffed animal from the floor and stood there hugging it to his chest and looking guilty.

"I'm sorry, Ms. Brannigan." He couldn't quite meet her eyes.

Her heart softened, knowing the boy had been through a lot over the last month. But still. He couldn't be allowed to get into fights to solve his problems. "I don't think it's me you need to apologize to, Bobby."

"I know." His tone and his sigh sounded much older than his years. He turned to face Hailey. "I'm sorry I called you a baby." He held out the purple dragon as a peace offering. "He's a really cool dragon."

Hailey snatched him back a little too quickly to be polite. "Thanks," she said, hugging Draco tight to her chest and drew in a deep breath. "Have you been to the Vampire Room to get candy yet?"

"There's a Vampire Room?" Bobby's face lit up. "Do they have real vampires handing out candy?"

"Nah, it's my Gramps in charge," Hailey confided, a smile on her face. "In real life, he's a teacher at the high school."

"That's cool! Where is he?"

"Come with me," Hailey said, grabbing his hand and pulling him down the hall toward one of the classrooms.

And just like that, the fight was forgotten.

Erin picked up the matching plastic helmets from the hallway floor and followed at a slower pace. Other parents and children greeted her as she passed through the crowds, and though she was friendly she didn't linger to chat. She wanted to keep an eye on the pair of knights who ran on ahead. She needed to make sure their tentative truce held, at least for the remainder of the night.

Monday on the playground? Who knows what will happen.

Even as she followed in their wake, she wondered where Bobby's grandmother was and why she'd let him out of her sight for so long. In the few interactions she'd had with the woman, Agnes struck Erin and something of a control freak. So how was Bobby wanderin the Community Center alone?

She paused at the doorway where a posted sign claimed *"Caution! Vampires Inside."* Like the hallways, the overhead lights in the room were covered in orange cellophane. Spiderwebs woven from grey yarn dangled from window frames and corners, and a fog machine in the corner whirred, sending white fog crawling across the tiled floor.

A hundred plastic bats dangled and swayed from the ceiling on fishing line. Black cloth covered the long table in the center of the room, pooling on the floor and seeming to disappear into the swirling fog. A plain pinewood coffin sat in the center, overflowing with candy and assorted plastic trinkets

Hailey and Bobby stood side by side atop chairs pushed up next to the table, digging into the coffin's treasure under the watchful eye of Erin's father, the three of them chatting like old friends. As if the fight had never happened. Her dad looked over at her and winked, unaware there had been any drama at all.

Kids, she thought, shaking her head. *If only grownups could fight and make up as easily.*

"There you are!"

Erin turned at the familiar voice laced with unfamiliar levels of stress. Zack strode into the room, his long legs eating up the space. The little girl on his shoulders wore black from head to toe, including a scarf that covered half of her head and had two uneven eye holes cut into it, too small to see out properly. For a full minute, Erin tried to decide what the girl's costume was supposed to be.

"Bobby, I told you not to wander away from us," Zack scolded, completely oblivious to Erin's presence in the room.

"But Karly was taking too long playing that stupid ghost bowling game," Bobby told him, not taking his eyes off the treasure-box coffin. "I wanted to get to the good stuff faster."

"We talked about this in the car," Zack said, huffing out a breath, looking like he was clinging to his sanity by a thread. "About sticking together because there's so many people here tonight." He laid his hand on Bobby's shoulder, and noticed the red mark on the boy's neck. His eyes went wide. "What the hell happened here?"

Bobby shrugged off Zack's hand, tkaing a step back. "Hailey and I had a fight. Now we're friends."

"What do you mean you had a fight? Where? When? Who is Henry?"

Erin decided it was time to interject. "*Hailey,* not Henry, is my daughter," she told him as she pushed away from the wall and stepped up beside him. "They've already worked it out between them."

Zack spun to face her, a look of surprise on his face. The girl on his shoulders let out a squeal.

"Uncle Z! Uncle Z! Lemme down!" Karly insisted, drumming on the top of his head with both hands until he reached up and pulled her up over his head, depositing her on the floor in front of him.

Erin went down on one knee to pull the black scarf off the girl's head. "I think it'll be easier to choose candy if you can see the choices."

Karly gave her a wide smile. "Thanks," she said before scurrying over to join her big brother.

"You have a daughter?" Zack asked, the disbelieving look still on his face.

Erin ignored the questions and handed the mask and one of the knight helmets to Zack. "Kids her age really shouldn't have a mask like that."

"Like what?"

"One she can't see out of. And Bobby's cape is a safety hazard too. I told him that yesterday at school, and made him keep it in his cubby so he wouldn't get hurt. I also mentioned to his grandmother at the end-of-day pickup that if Bobby wanted to wear a cape she should sew it onto his costume."

Zack's eyebrows pulled together, his mouth dipping into a frown. "She didn't say anything to me before she left."

"Left?"

"She and Richard flew home to Florida last night."

"But I thought…" Erin glanced over at Bobby and Karly.

"No. I'm their guardian."

A surge of shocked surprise ran through her. "You?"

His eyebrows drew together again. "What's that supposed to mean?"

"What do you know about raising kids?"

"Ha! That's rich, coming from the woman whose kid nearly strangled my nephew."

"Yes, but…"

Zack held up a hand to stop her protests, and stepped forward to scoop Karly into his arms, shoving her headscarf and the knight helmet into her goodie bag. He grabbed Bobby by the hand. "Come on, kids, we're leaving."

"But we haven't trick-or-treated in all the rooms yet," Bobby whined, dragging behind his uncle, trying to dig his heels into the tiled floor.

Erin watched the three of them leave, a pang of sympathy clutching at her chest. Not only for the unhappy kids, but for Zack as well. He seemed to be way out of his depth, if the frantic look on his face when he'd first found Bobby was any indication.

She couldn't believe Agnes and Richard left, leaving Zack to flounder on his own. Then again, the man ran a successful business and navigated adventures around the world for his television show. To the viewing audience, he seemed like a pro at facing every kind of dangerous situation with confidence and skill.

Erin hoped he'd be able to navigate this latest adventure with the same expertise.

But she had her doubts.

"Who was that?"

Her mother had snuck up on her. Before answering, Erin looked over to make sure Hailey was still occupied with her grandfather, helping hand out candy to other trick-or-treaters.

"Zack Donovan. Uncle to Bobby Mills, whose parents just died last month."

Her mother frowned. "I thought Agnes and Robert moved back to town to take care of their grandkids. No?"

"Apparently not," Erin told her. "Zack said they left yesterday."

"Huh." Her mother's frown disappeared as she snapped her fingers. "Hey wait a minute! Wasn't he the boy you had a crush on all through high school? Scribbling his name on all your notebooks?"

"Mom!" More than mortified, Erin grabbed her mother's arm and tugged. "Keep your voice down!"

"Pffft. No one cares about ancient history," her mother told her, yanking her arm out of Erin's hold and patting her cheek. "Not nearly as exciting as being pursued by a prince."

"What are you talking about?"

"Did you see the flowers on the dining room table?"

Yes, she'd seen the overly large bouquet of fall splendor as soon as she'd walked into the house after work. A gorgeous arrangement of mums, carnations, seasonal greens, and fall color that screamed expensive. "Dad really outdid himself with those."

"They aren't from Dad."

She smiled at her mother. "No? You have a rich secret admirer you want to tell me about?"

Her mother smiled right back. "No, I don't. But you do. Those are from Leo."

Erin's brow crinkled. "Leo?"

"Leo Kensington? Hailey's father?"

She huffed, her heart beating a fast staccato in her chest. "I know which Leo you meant. But why?"

"The card says, *Call me*. I'm guessing he wants to talk with you before he comes to visit his daughter." Her mother patted her arm. "I'm in also guessing that means you haven't called him back yet."

Erin's eyes shifted away. "I haven't had the time."

"Make the time." There was steel in her mother's voice.

"Mom…":

"Listen. It would be one thing if you were happy. But I know you, Erin, and you're not. You moved home for Hailey's sake, but you've been in limbo for the last seven years. Waiting for your life to start again."

"Mom…"

Maureen held up a hand like a stop sign. "I know I overstepped when I invited that man to spend Christmas with our family. But I'm not going to apologize again. You need to talk with him. You need to figure out what it is you want out of life."

Erin bristled. "I love being a mom. I enjoy teaching. I love Cape Cod."

Her mother nodded in agreement. "But is it enough?"

Erin opened her mouth, but no words came out. Because she didn't know the answer.

CHAPTER 5

November

*"*W*hat do you know about raising kids?"*

For the last few weeks, Erin Brannigan's words had been running on repeat in Zack's head. Her words... and her curves if he was being honest with himself. The softness of her body was in stark contrast to the steel of her voice. And to the tantalizing fire that flashed in her blue eyes when she'd told him about Bobby's fight with her daughter. She was like a puzzle he wanted to solve, an adventure he couldn't resist.

But she thought he was unfit to raise his nephew and niece.

"What do you know about raising kids?"

He heard her disparaging words in his head constantly. Every time Karly melted down getting ready for school. Every time the two kids got into screaming matches over what show to watch after dinner. Every time he was late to school pickup, and Bobby was the last kid standing there on the sidewalk.

Like today.

He was late again today.

How did his sister ever do all of this by herself? He knew his brother-in-law traveled constantly for work, and yet Daphne always seemed to have everything under control. Always.

Zack felt like he was constantly twelve steps behind.

He tried to be on time, he really did. And yet somehow... between laundry and naptime and grocery shopping and soccer for Bobby and cleaning the house and ballet for Karly and trying to squeeze in a few work calls, the time disappeared. Poof. Gone.

How did Daphne do all this and stay sane?

Maybe it was easier if a parent got to start with the kid as a baby, before they could voice opinions or opposition, before they had to be driven around town to school and sports and other various activities. Or maybe it would be easier if he wasn't trying to figure out how to salvage his television show and his travel company while taking care of two small children all on his own, now that their grandparents returned to Florida. Why was it he'd fought with Agnes to leave?

His travel company wasn't the issue. The team was chugging along, bookings projections looking better than ever. He'd already expanded over the last year, hiring additional staff and tour guides to keep up with demand generated by the success of his TV show.

Epic Adventures made him a star. Not quite a household name, but scores of fans watched the cable show and followed Zack on social media, the audience growing each year. Before the trip to South Africa, he'd been talking with a larger network to take the show to the next level, since the current contract only ran through one more season. The episodes airing this fall had been shot last year, and his South African shark adventure was part of the spring season of shows that they'd almost finished filming before... well, before.

All those plans were on hold now, and Zack didn't see any way to reconcile his old life with his new reality.

"What do you know about raising kids?"

Erin's voice in his head brought him back from his internal musings. Bobby and Karly were the most important things in his life right now, and he needed to keep them front and center in his mind.

He pulled into the elementary school parking lot and saw a few cars still inching along the curb in the pick-up line in front of him. Even though he might be last in line – the very, very last – the line was still there, winding toward the designated pick-up area.

"Are we late again, Uncle Z?" Karly's car seat sat directly behind the driver, so her very loud question was right in his ear and her kicking reverberated through the driver's seat directly into his spine.

"Not late today," he said, catching her eye in the rearview mirror, the minivan creeping forward slowly but surely.

"Are we last ones here again?"

"Maybe?"

Karly giggled and started singing. "Last one left is the rotten egg. Bobby's the rotten e-e-e-gg."

Zack rolled his eyes. "Cut that out, kiddo. Be nice."

"What do you know about raising kids?"

Zack shook his head, trying to dispel the mocking question. Easy enough for someone like her to be judgmental, when she probably had a husband at home to help out. He grimaced at the thought of Erin happily married, not sure why that made his stomach grumble unhappily.

On top of having Mr. Perfect by her side, Erin was a teacher, so of course she knew everything about raising kids. She'd probably learned it all in college getting her teaching degree. Not a chance he could ever measure up to any of it.

When it was finally his turn, he pulled close to the curb and lowered the window, wincing when he saw Erin Brannigan herself standing with her hand on his nephew's shoulder. Again. No doubt judging him on his inability to perform a simple task like picking up his nephew on time.

Pasting on a smile, he hit the automatic door button on what he continued to think of as Daphne's minivan. "Hey Bobby! Hop in!"

Bobby didn't move from his teacher's side.

Erin cleared her throat and bended her knees to meet his eyes through the open door. "Mr. Donovan? Do you have a minute to chat?"

"Gosh, Ms. Brannigan, now is not a good time for us. I need to get Bobby home to change into his soccer clothes and get him over to the Community Center for his game. Another time maybe?"

Instead of answering, she turned to Bobby. "What soccer team are you on?"

"We're the red team, but we named ourselves Red Blaze," the boy said. "Can I go now?"

"Of course. Good luck in your game, Bobby." She took a step back and watched as he climbed into the car and buckled the seatbelt by himself. Only then did her eyes raise to meet Zack's again. "I look forward to seeing you soon, Mr. Donovan."

Zack kept the false smile splashed across his face as he hit the close button for the door – *thank god for automatic doors* – and mumbled "Not if I see you first." Childish? Maybe. But he already heard enough of Erin's condemnation every day in his head. He didn't need to hear it in person, too.

AN HOUR LATER, he stood on the sidelines reading email on his phone as the U6 soccer teams warmed up before the start of the game. Karly sat nearby on a beach towel, coloring with crayons on a sketch pad. Bobby's coach had set out little orange cones in a box pattern and the kids were trying to dribble from one to the next without kicking too hard and losing their soccer balls. A nice idea, but in reality there were balls and kids in red shirts all over the entire field, including mingling with the opposing team who were dressed all in purple, and doing pretty much the same drills with the same amount of chaos.

At least they're evenly matched.

Zack glanced down again and re-read the latest email from his friend and cameraman one more time, trying to figure out a way to answer Mike that wouldn't sound like total bullshit.

His mind was a blank.

It seemed that even with stretching all of the footage they'd already shot, they were still one full episode short for the upcoming season. Their contract called for ten shows, and right now there were only nine of them, no matter how much Mike tried to squeeze every last minute out of the footage he'd shot on their most recent trips to Australia, Switzerland, Fiji, and that last one to South Africa. They'd had to cancel the filming in Kenya, which would have been the season finale.

Every night for the last few weeks Zack watched the rough cuts late into the evenings, after Bobby and Karly were asleep. Long hours spent recording commentary of nature facts and a little regional history to be dubbed in to accompany the underwater shots and scenery footage. Koalas and kangaroos might not look as dangerous as Great White Sharks, but they still needed to be treated with care and respect. This was nothing new for him, he always overdubbed the background shots, and loved the researching of facts to share with his viewers, but this time seemed different.

Like he was trying to stretch out the video footage as far as it would go.

Which was the truth.

One more episode? How? I can't leave the kids now. He frowned at his phone screen a minute longer, before tapping out a reply that he'd think of something to appease the network and fulfill the terms of the contract.

He had to. It was his show. His team.

The crew depended on him.

Then again, so did Bobby and Karly. He was all they had now.

"Mr. Donovan, we meet again. Do you think you might have a moment to talk now?"

Zack looked up from his phone to find Erin Brannigan standing in front of him, arms crossed over her chest. The determined look on her face made him smirk.

"Are you here to harass me about being late for school pick-up? Don't you have better things to do with your afternoon?"

"As it happens, my daughter plays on the purple team," she said with a nod to the opposite end of the soccer field. "And I'm not here to harass, I'm only trying to help."

"Help?" His tone might have been skeptical, but part of him was screaming *Yes, please*! The last few weeks he'd felt like a hamster on a treadmill, constantly running but never gaining ground. Between the late nights working on the show and the early mornings trying to wrangle two small humans out the door to school, Zack felt like he was running on empty.

He knew he needed help... but he wasn't sure he wanted it from the woman standing in front of him.

"For instance, three o'clock seems to be an issue for you..." Erin started diplomatically.

"You mean I'm constantly late," Zack corrected, staring her down.

Calm blue eyes remained locked with his. "You probably don't know this because your sister didn't need it. But. The elementary school offers an after-hours session for working parents, where the kids can hang out and do their homework or play board games until someone comes to pick them up. It's supervised and available up until 6:00, and the fees are very reasonable. You need to apply and it'll take a week or two to get approved, but then you're golden. They also have morning care, if you need to drop Bobby off before first bell, but that doesn't seem to be your problem time."

When Zack didn't immediately jump at the idea, Erin added, "My daughter goes after school most days, to play with the other kids while I get errands done. It's hard on a single parent to squeeze in the time to get everything accomplished and still feel like you're being present for your child. Or in your case, children."

He knew he should be asking for more details about this after-school session thing – which actually sounded like the answer to a prayer – but the first question out of his mouth was, "You're not married?"

"Uh, no," she told him, looking as surprised at the question as Zack was that he'd asked it.

"Were you married?"

"Never," she said. "Which isn't relevant to..."

"Where is Hailey's father?"

"I'm not sure how that's any of your business," Erin said, confusion – *and maybe embarrassment?* – plain on her face.

And maybe technically it wasn't his business, Zack allowed. But since fighting with Hailey on Halloween, Bobby had developed a complete fascination with everything about Erin's perfect daughter and talked about her constantly, from her purple stuffed dragon (*"Why can't I have a dragon too?"*) to the fact she took Tae Kwon Do on Saturday mornings (*"Can Karly and I sign up for lessons?"*) and everything in between. Zack felt like he knew so much about the little blonde girl... and yet he didn't know Erin was a single mom.

He needed to know more. Staring at her now, seeing those blue eyes darken the longer he stared, something inside him stirred.

"Uncle Z! Uncle Z!" Bobby's sweaty body rammed into his uncle's leg, arms wrapping tight around his thigh like one of those koalas from the last Australian adventure. "Where's my water bottle?"

Zack looked down, realizing his mistake instantly. "Shi...itake mushrooms. I left it on the kitchen counter. Sorry, buddy."

Bobby's face contorted in disappointment but before he could respond, Erin was rifling through the oversized bag hanging on her shoulder, pulling out a water bottle.

"Here you go," she said as she handed him a reusable plastic bottle with the elementary school logo on it.

Zack shook his head, voicing his protest even as Bobby grabbed for the water. "We can't take your daughter's bottle."

"It's an extra," Erin said, the corners of her mouth turning up. "I learned early on someone always forgets. And we've got a ready supply of extra logo bottles in the teacher lounge."

"Thanks, Mrs. B.," Bobby said, wiping the drips from his face and taking the bottle with him back to where his team now huddled together around the coach.

Zack cocked an eyebrow at her. "Mrs.?"

"Nope. I already told you. Not married." Erin swung the canvas bag off her shoulder, dropping it to the ground by her feet.

"But..."

Erin turned to scan the soccer field as she spoke. The two teams were getting set up on the field, taking their places for the initial kick-off. "Kindergarteners find it easier. They always confuse the *"Ms."* with *"Mrs."* I don't bother to correct them."

"But where…"

"He didn't want kids. Took himself out of the picture before she was born."

"I'm sorry."

"I'm not. He showed his true colors and we're better off without him."

From the bitterness of her tone, Zack knew there was more to that story but wasn't about to demand details. *None of my business, like she said.* Except. He burned with curiosity. For some reason, he *wanted* it to be his business. He wanted to know more about the woman standing at his side.

And wasn't that a kick in the balls.

Zack cleared his throat. "The after-school program sounds perfect for us. Especially while I'm trying to finalize the spring season."

Erin didn't hide her surprise. "You're still filming *Epic Adventures*?"

"Technically, we've already done all the filming," he told her, smiling at the look on her face. He remembered her telling him she loved his show, that day at his sister's funeral. Right before he basically accused her of hitting on him and called her a cheap slut.

His smile faded from his lips. He needed to apologize.

Before he could get the words out of his mouth, a commotion rose on the field. He turned to see all the kids from both teams crowded around one of the goals. The kids wearing purple were jumping up and down, but Zack's gaze zeroed in on Bobby and another of his red-shirted teammates pushing each other and exchanging what looked like angry words.

Erin ran onto the field toward her child, who sat on the ground holding her leg. Zack headed straight for Bobby. The coach got there first, standing between the two boys, hands on his hips, as the boys continued to argue with him and point at each other. Another parent also joined them, putting his hand on the other boy's shoulder.

"What happened?" Zack asked when he reached the group.

Bobby turned to him, jabbing a finger at his teammate. "Nate kicked Hailey in the leg and knocked her down."

"I was trying to kick the ball away from the goal," the other boy protested, looking up at the guy standing next to him. "Just like you showed me, right Dad?"

"You hurt my friend," Bobby yelled. "You kicked her on purpose!"

"It was an acc - i - dent!" Nate yelled back, emphasizing each syllable.

"But you kicked her after she passed the ball to Kyle," Bobby insisted. "I saw you!"

"Boys," the coach said in a placating voice. "We're all on the same team here. This is supposed to be fun. Can you apologize to each other and let's get on with the game?"

Zack pulled Bobby away from the argument and turned him to face away from the other boy. Bending down to look him in the eye, he asked, "Are you okay? I thought Nate was your friend."

"Hailey's my friend too. And Nate kicked her on purpose." Bobby crossed his arms over his chest and stared defiantly at Zack.

"She got in my way," Nate protested again.

"It's all part of the game," the other father said, ruffling his son's hair. "Maybe if the girl can't take a kick, she shouldn't be playing soccer with the boys."

"They're in kindergarten," Zack said, straightening to his full height, which he was glad to see was a few inches taller than the other dad. "They're here to run around and have fun."

"The only fun is in winning," the guy, his eyes narrowing. "You should understand that, Mr. Big Shot Television Star. I'm sure you didn't get your own show by playing nice."

The coach shook his head, frowning. "We've been through this before, Mr. Petersen. The under-six teams are mixed. Boys and girls playing together to learn the basics of the sport."

"If you're not going to teach them to be competitive, then maybe we need to find another team." He grabbed his son's hand and pulled him toward the parking lot, bending his head to talk to him as they walked.

Zack bit back the retort on the tip of his tongue about teaching his son about playing fair. The fact was he didn't see what happened on the field, so he couldn't say for sure whether the kick was accidental or not. But the guy's attitude was all kinds of wrong for so many reasons. The kids were only in kindergarten, for fuck's sake. Not trying to win the World Cup. And what was with the casual misogyny? Was that really something the guy wanted to teach his child?

He shook it off and focused on Bobby. "Are you okay?" he asked again.

Bobby nodded, hands still in fists, the corners of his mouth dipping low as he whispered, "Am I in trouble?"

"For defending your friend Hailey? Never," Zack assured him, and the surliness disappeared from the boy's face. "For fighting with your teammate? That's up to your coach."

The coach put his hands on his hips, his gaze on the parking lot. "Looks like Nate and his dad are really leaving." He looked down at Bobby. "If you can promise me no more fighting on the field, you can stay and play the rest of the game."

"I promise, Coach Joe."

"Okay then. Get back over there with the team. I need a word with your uncle."

Bobby ran off, and Zack turned his attention to the coach. "Thanks for letting him stay in the game, Coach Joe."

"Bobby was right, it was a late kick." The coach rolled his eyes. "At this age, these things happen all the time. It's part of the game. And I don't think the girl was seriously injured."

They both looked over to the purple sidelines, where Hailey was jumping around with her teammates as if nothing had happened.

"I have no idea if Nate kicked her on purpose, so I didn't want to make a big deal," Joe said, his voice not much above a whisper. "But honestly? The team will be better off without Dave Petersen yelling his negative bullshit from the sidelines." He cocked his head and squinted at Zack. "You don't remember me, do you?"

Taken aback, Zack looked at him more closely. "Ummm…"

"Joe Wheeler. I was two grades ahead of you in school, on the soccer team. I know you played lacrosse instead, so we didn't interact too much. For what it's worth, I'm wicked sorry about Daphne and Robert."

"Thanks." Zack felt like an idiot for not recognizing the guy before now. He'd let Agnes take care of playing soccer mom for most of the season, only showing up on the sidelines for the last two weeks. But still.

"It's a good thing you're doing, taking on the role of guardian for those two kids. They need you."

Zack shrugged. "My sister did it for me."

"Yeah, I remember that from high school. If you need anything – a playdate, or just someone to whine to – my wife and I were friendly with your sister and Robert, and my youngest son Jack is in Bobby's class. You can call us anytime."

A lump formed in Zack's throat, making it hard to push out words. Since Agnes and Richard left at the end of October, he'd been on his own with the kids. "Thanks, man. Appreciate the offer."

Joe clapped a hand on his back. "I mean it. Anytime. Parenting isn't for the faint of heart. Not that it's exactly the same as the adventures you go on for your television show, but it's not a simple walk in the park either. Sometimes it's more like *Jurassic Park*."

Zack barked out a surprised laugh. "That's for damn sure."

"Hey, if you're not doing anything this coming Saturday, a bunch of us guys are getting together at my house for the afternoon with the kids. Kids play in the yard, we watch a little college ball, everyone eats some pizza at the end of the day. We get together at least once a month, give the moms a break, like a moms-night-out kinda thing but for a whole Saturday. I know you're a big shot TV star and all, but you wanna join us?"

Zack didn't hesitate to grab the lifeline Joe offered. "Actually, that sounds pretty great."

CHAPTER 6

"You sure you're good to keep playing?" Erin rubbed her hand across the large red welt already forming on Hailey's shin before helping her to her feet. There would be an impressive bruise by the morning.

"I'm not a baby, Mom," Hailey said in a matter-of-fact voice. "Getting kicked is part of playing soccer. Coach Alison tells us that all the time."

"Okay. If you're sure." Erin reluctantly let go of her daughter's hand and watched her run over to the sidelines to high five the teammate who scored the goal off Hailey's assist. She saw Zack with Bobby and the red team coach, and watched Dave Petersen walk his son off the field.

Tamping down on the urge to follow him to the parking lot and make Nate come back to apologize, she returned to where her bag sat on the sidelines near Karly. The preschooler was lying stomach down on her beach towel, coloring in her notepad, oblivious to the drama on the field or the fact her uncle ran off and left her alone.

Erin sighed. One child at a time was enough to worry about. She didn't envy Zack the position his sister left him in, and had to admit he was probably doing better than many other single guys would do in the same place.

She squatted next to Karly and picked up one of the discarded pages, fully covered with colorful scribbles and symbols in messy rows. "What are you drawing, sweetie?"

"I'm writing, not drawing," she said, her little pink tongue poking out one side of her mouth as she concentrated. "Bobby said we need to start our Santa lists. So I'm practicing."

"Good thinking. Do you know what you want for Christmas?"

Karly tipped her head to look up at her, a serious look on her little face. "Bobby told me I can't ask for Mommy and Daddy to come home from Heaven. So instead I'm asking if Santa will tell Zack to stay with us forever."

Erin's heart squeezed so hard she thought it might burst. "I'm not sure that's a wish Santa can grant for you, sweetheart."

Karly nodded. "Grandma said the same thing on the phone when I told her last night. She said not to worry because she and Grandpa will be coming at Christmas to bring us to live with them, instead of staying here with Uncle Z."

Which didn't surprise Erin. Zack had to return to his real life at some point. "Your grandparents love you very much. They probably miss you."

The little girl frowned. "I guess so. But I'd rather live in my house than in Florida. And Uncle Z is more fun. He plays with me. And listens to me. If I can't have Mommy and Daddy back, I want him to stay. Even if we're always late to everything, and he turned all the laundry pink last week because of Bobby's soccer shirt."

"I'm sure he's doing his best to figure it out," Erin told her. She had no idea whether Zack wanted to stay or was counting down the days until the grandparents returned. She decided it might be safer to change the subject, redirecting the girl's attention back to the paper in front of her. "What toys are you asking Santa for this year?

Karly shrugged and concentrated on choosing a fresh crayon. "Maybe I'll ask for a new bike to ride in the neighborhood next summer. I'm too big for my tricycle. But it has to be blue like Bobby's, or maybe green. I don't want a pink bike like Anna who lives up the block. Just because I'm a girl doesn't mean I should always get pink. Even if Uncle Z turned all my socks and underwear pink."

Marveling at how quickly the girl shifted gears, Erin suggested she draw the bike so Santa could see what color she wanted. Erin watched her, wondered if Karly would be riding her new bike in Chatham next summer, or in Florida. If Zack couldn't figure out how to step up, he was going to lose that battle to his sister's in-laws. Apparently Christmas was the deadline for him to get his act together.

Zack wasn't the only one with a Christmas deadline.

Leo Kensington would be coming to spend Christmas on Cape Cod.

The night before, Leo's travel agent finally forwarded an itinerary, making it real. Leo planned to arrive on Hailey's birthday, December 15, and stay through New Year's Day. Two full weeks. Staying at the Atlantic Inn right on the shoreline, the most expensive hotel in town.

After getting over the shock that the visit was really happening, Erin finally called him back.

And got her second shock of the day.

Leo apologized.

Apologized! After seven years! As if a handful of nice words in his posh accent could dull the pain of what he'd done. He kicked her out of their shared flat and studio space for having the audacity of becoming pregnant! It's not like she got in that condition all on her own, after all.

Then again, that was more than seven years ago. She was happy with her life now, and more than happy to have Hailey in her life.

She'd hesitated for a moment, but accepted the apology. For Hailey's sake, if nothing else. Christmas would be awkward enough with Leo here in Chatham for the first time ever. They didn't need any lingering resentment or ill feelings muddying the first holiday the kid got to spend with her father.

Then he gave her the third shock of the day.

Leo offered to move her back to England, to live with him in Surrey. She and Hailey both. To be a "real family," as he put it. He claimed to miss her. To want the chance to know their daughter better, and help raise her. In the wake of her silence, he asked how she felt about the idea.

Stunned was the only word to describe it.

Shocked would be another good word.

"Hell no" were the words that actually came out of her mouth, before she'd hung up on him. And spent the night and most of the day avoiding any thoughts of Leo and his out-of-the-blue offer.

"Hey, thanks for hanging out with Karly," Zack said, jogging up along the sidelines to rejoin them, jarring her from her thoughts of Leo and his out-of-the-blue offers. "Everything okay with your daughter?"

"She claims she's fine, that getting kicked like you're in an MMA cage fight is part of the game," Erin told him. "I didn't see what happened though, did you?"

Zack shook his head. "Bobby said Nate did it on purpose. That's what the boys were fighting about."

"Oh." Erin frowned. "I didn't realize there was a fight."

"Dave Petersen is..." Zack paused and glanced down at Karly. "Well, he was kind of a d-i-c-k about the whole thing and ended up taking his son off the team."

"Nate isn't in my class but I've heard rumors in the teacher's lounge. The Petersens are not anyone's favorite parents to deal with."

"Yeah, I got that impression after one short interaction. I'm glad Hailey's okay." One corner of Zack's mouth hitched upward into a half smile, sending a tingle zinging up her spine. The good kind of tingle. The kind she shouldn't be feeling around Bobby's parent. Except he wasn't really a parent.

But I shouldn't be feeling it regardless, she told herself.

He looked down at Karly again before meeting her eyes. "You said before that you're a single parent. If it's just you and Hailey, when do you get a break?"

Startled by the abrupt change in subject, she stared at him unable to respond for almost a full minute, Leo's offer of a "real family" roaring back into her head. "I... I don't know what you mean."

Zack hooked a thumb over his shoulder. "Joe Wheeler invited me and the kids over for a playdate Saturday, and it's apparently a thing they do once a month to give their wives some time for themselves."

Erin squared her shoulders. "I've heard about the monthly *Moms' Day Out*." She'd even been invited once or twice by other Chatham moms that she knew from her high school days. That was when Hailey was younger, and she'd been busy with classes at the community college to earn her teaching degree and figure out a new plan for her life. She must have said "no" one too many times and the invites stopped coming.

"So, I was thinking if you could help me expedite getting Bobby signed up for the afterschool program so he can start this coming Monday, then I'd be happy to pick Hailey up and take her with us to Joe's this Saturday. That way you can get a day off and do the moms' day thing."

She frowned. "Are you trying to blackmail me to get Bobby into a program he's already eligible for?"

Zack smiled and spread his hands wide. "Blackmail is such an ugly word. I prefer to think of it as friends helping each other out. You scratch my back, I scratch yours. I need that afterschool program as soon as possible, and I think you could probably use some adult time as much as I do."

Erin thought about it, trying to figure out the catch. Sure, he wanted her help to get Bobby signed up faster than the usual process, but she probably would've offered that anyway.

"Why?"

"Why what?"

"Why are you being nice to me now?" Erin stared into those sparkling grey eyes, trying to figure out his motivation. Every interaction they'd had in since he'd returned to Chatham ended with harsh words. What changed?

"Honestly?" Zack pushed his fingers through his hair, making his dark curls stand on end in a sexy disheveled sort of way. She imagined it would look much the same first thing in the morning, his head still on his pillow as he smiled over at her. She blinked hard, trying to push away the distracting image.

Zack was still explaining. "I'm tired of trying to do it all on my own. I know I need help if I'm going to do this guardian thing without screwing the kids up for life. And... I could use a friend."

The honesty of his tone hit her square in the chest and his smile did funny things to her insides. It felt like a host of butterflies had suddenly taken up residence in her belly, fluttering like crazy.

"Okay."

Zack blinked. "Okay what?"

I'll be your friend. With benefits. "I'll get Bobby into the after-school program starting on Monday. You can pick Hailey up on Saturday and take her with you to Joe's house."

"Really?"

"Really."

"That's great!" He threw his arms around her for a hug, pressing that hard body against hers.

After her earlier awareness of him, Zack's friendly gesture overwhelmed her senses. Erin inhaled his spicy musk, closing her eyes briefly to breathe him in. How long had it been since she'd been held like this? She found herself circling her arms around his waist to return the hug, oddly reluctant to let go. After what could have been a few seconds, a few minutes, or a few hours, she forced herself to step away from him before she did something she couldn't take back.

Like kissing the shit out of him.

For a moment he seemed as flustered and unsure as she felt, before reverting to the cocky grin he'd made famous on his television show. "So, I was thinking..."

Before he could finish his sentence, the rest of the crowd erupted in cheers. Zack and Erin both looked to the other end of the field, where the red team were jumping and cheering.

One of the other soccer moms stepped closer to them. "Congrats on Bobby's goal, Zack! His first of the season! You must be a wonderful influence on him."

Zack grinned at the other mom. "Thanks, Stephanie. But really, it's all him. I don't know much about soccer, as you probably remember from our high school days."

Erin couldn't help but glare at the other woman. Stephanie Ruhle. Redhead, vivacious, and still as popular as she was in high school. She and her perfectly perky tits were on the cheer squad, and in their graduating class.

No wonder Zack remembered her.

That's not fair, the little voice in her head argued. *He remembered you right away. He remembered your plan to move to Europe, too.*

"Stephanie, you know Erin Brannigan, right?" Zack turned halfway to include her in the conversation.

"Hey there Erin! My Fiona is in Ms. Wilson's room this year, but I know you teach one of the other kindergarten classes."

"Oh, I know Fiona. Everyone knows Fiona." Erin resisted the urge to roll her eyes. Not only was the little girl the spitting image of her mom, but also the loudest kid on the playground every day at recess, always yelling about something or at someone. Unfortunately, many times that *someone* ended up being Hailey, another highly opinionated kindergartener in Mrs. Wilson's classroom. Erin knew it would serve both girls well in their futures, to be able to stand up for themselves and have strong opinions, but as a teacher it made recess.... Interesting. To say the least.

Stephanie chuckled, waving a hand in the air as if to disperse a bad smell. "I know, I know. But redheads come by their tempers honestly. We've been working hard on inside versus outside voices this year."

"That's... good to hear," Erin said diplomatically.

Stephanie's gaze ping ponged between the two of them. "Are either of you planning to attend the high school reunion next weekend? I know they closed our old school building when the town regionalized with Harwich, but they're having a reunion thing at the new high school on the Saturday after Thanksgiving. Like a prom for grownups, for all the reunion-year classes from both Harwich and Chatham, you know, ten years, fifteen years, twenty, twenty five and so on... which includes our class."

Zack looked at Erin. "Were you thinking of going?"

She nodded. "I heard about it. My parents are okay with babysitting for the night. I just hadn't decided for sure whether I was going to attend."

Zack grinned. "I'll go if you go."

"I have nothing fancy to wear for a prom," Erin countered.

"A group of us are going off-Cape on Saturday to shop the outlets," Stephanie said. "You're welcome to join us." She rattled off a bunch of familiar names, women they'd gone to school with, and where they planned to meet.

"Saturday? I'm not sure..." It clicked in Erin's mind. Moms' Day Out, and Zack offering to take Hailey for the afternoon. "Actually, that sounds like fun, if Zack can pick up Hailey for that playdate a little earlier?" She turned to the him as she asked the question.

"Not a problem," he assured her.

Stephanie's eyes held a speculative gleam. "Are you two..."

"Friends," Erin answered quickly, cutting her off before she finished the sentence. "Just friends."

CHAPTER 7

Zack shifted Karly higher on his hip before ringing the doorbell of the sprawling house. He wondered what it was that Joe did for a living, besides coaching U6 soccer, to afford such a large house on the edge of town and abutting conservation land. He glanced behind him at Bobby and Hailey. They were deep in a discussion about some movie they'd both seen recently. "You guys are on your best behavior today, understand? This is a really nice house and I don't want you breaking anything."

"Sure, Uncle Z. I've been here before."

"When?"

"Jack's birthday party last summer." Bobby turned to Hailey, excited. "He's got an awesome treehouse in his backyard, and a trampoline too. We can see who can bounce highest!"

Which sounded not at all safe. Before Zack could squash that idea, the door opened.

Joe greeted them all with a smile. "Come on in," he said, ushering them into the house.

Kid-sized coats, shoes, and stuffed canvas tote bags sat in a pile near the door. Joe pointed left toward the oversized great room. "Bobby, if you and Hailey want to leave your shoes on and go through that sliding door, the rest of the big kids are out in the yard choosing teams for kickball."

Hailey offered the large Tupperware she'd brought from home. "Coach Joe, my mom and I baked these last night to say thank you for inviting us."

He accepted the container, cracking the lid to take a peek. "Chocolate chip cookies? How'd you know they're my favorite?"

"Aren't they everyone's favorite?"

"Thanks for these. I'll add them to the snacks in the kitchen. Now you two should go join the kickball squad." Joe gestured to the sliding door again.

Bobby and Hailey looked at each other and took off at a run.

"No running in the house," Zack called after them.

Joe chuckled. "Don't worry about it. I put my oldest in charge of wearing out the younger kids before we serve lunch. And what's this little one's name?" He tickled Karly's chin, making her plaster her face against Zack's shoulder and neck.

"This is Karly. She's feeling a little shy today." Zack tried to nudge her away from his side but she clung tighter than that koala he'd held on his last journey into the Australian outback.

"Perfectly all right. She can watch football with us... or if she changes her mind, we've got movies in the playroom. I think they just started watching the one with the redheaded princess who shoots arrows."

Karly perked up at the description of one of her favorite characters and squirmed in Zack's arms.

He smiled. "I think you got her attention. Where is the playroom?"

Joe nodded. "Follow me. I'll give you the nickel tour while we're at it."

He pointed out the kitchen, the bathrooms, and finally the magical playroom with a large screen television on the wall and more than a dozen kids who looked to be around Karly's age sitting and lying on the floor, transfixed by the movie's first musical number. Zack lowered Karly to the floor and she plopped herself down next to another girl her size to share an oversized pillow, already enthralled by the magic of animation and the power of a badass princess.

The men went back down the hall to the kitchen where Joe placed the container of cookies on the kitchen island and offered up drink choices.

"Just soda for me, thanks." Zack popped the top on the can, noting the towering stack of juice boxes and mountain of individual sized bags of chips on the counter next to the fridge. "You look well prepared."

Joe laughed. "We've done this a time or two. The snack-size chip thing I learned early on. And every time it gets bigger, more moms wanting in on the day off thing. Got the hot dogs ready to go on the grill in an hour or so, and plenty of grown-up snacks in the den. If you want to stay through the four o'clock game, you can chip in for the pizza later."

"Sounds great."

Joe clicked his beer bottle against Zack's soda can. "So, you and Erin Brannigan, huh? When did that start?"

"No, we're just friends," Zack said, repeating the words Erin used with Stephanie the other day at the soccer field, even if they didn't taste quite right in his mouth. Didn't matter how much he'd enjoyed the hug they shared, feeling her soft body pressed up against his. She was Bobby's teacher and he wasn't about to cross any lines.

Shit, up until the other day he wasn't even sure she liked him very much.

"Friends, huh? But you've got her kid here with you today. And I hear you're taking her to your high school reunion too."

He shook his head. "Single parents helping each other out. She wanted to go out shopping with the girls today, and her parents agreed to babysit for all three kids for the reunion night. It's a mutually beneficial arrangement."

"Mutually beneficial, huh?"

At Zack's glare, Joe laughed and threw up both hands. "All right, all right, I'll lay off speculating on your *arrangement*. How are things going with the kids? It must be so hard for them without their parents."

"The therapist says it'll take time to adjust. I talk with them about Daphne and Robert, and put out the pictures and photo albums, like the woman suggested. But they both have so much anger bottled up in those little bodies. Karly especially seems to have tantrums at the drop of a hat," Zack admitted. "And Bobby's gotten into a few fights. Well, you saw the one on the soccer field."

"And I'm sure the therapist tells you it's expected behavior." Joe patted Zack's shoulder. "You're doing a good thing. It takes time."

"Time we don't have," Zack grumbled, thinking of last night's call with Agnes. She called once a week to talk with the kids, and always seemed to catch them at their worst. "Their grandmother is threatening to take them home with her after Christmas."

Joe's eyes widened. "What? How does she think it's a good idea to take them away from their home and everything familiar?"

"She doesn't think I'm a fit guardian," Zack said, his voice almost a whisper. "And some days, I agree with her."

Joe threw an arm Zack and pulled him toward the living room. "We all have those days. That's why we help each other out. And have gatherings like this one. C'mon, let's go see what the guys are watching on the other television."

SEVERAL HOURS, two football games, and countless animated movies later, Zack piled three tired kids back into the minivan. Karly was already fast asleep as he buckled her into her car seat. In the third row of seats, Bobby and Hailey buckled their own seatbelts, whispering with each other.

"Uncle Z? Can Hailey sleep over tonight?"

"I don't think so, buddy." He pulled down the long driveway onto the road, heading toward the center of town.

"Why not? It's not a school night," Bobby argued. "And I have extra pajamas she can borrow. There's a new movie that comes out tonight on cable, on a channel she doesn't get at home."

Zack smiled at the simple logic of six-year-olds. "I don't think Hailey's mom will let her."

"Why not?" Bobby persisted.

"Well, for one thing, she's a girl and you're a boy," Zack told him, thinking that made it obvious.

"So what? She's my friend."

"Mom lets me do sleepovers, Mr. Z. Let's call her," Hailey suggested.

Tired of arguing, Zack hit the button on the steering wheel to pull up his phone. He'd added Erin's contact information into his favorites when he picked Hailey up that morning. She picked up after one ring, her voice coming through the car speakers. "Zack! We were just talking about you! Were your ears ringing, or... Wait, is everything okay with the kids?"

He heard noise in the background, and realized she was probably still out with the other mothers, probably having dinner or drinks out somewhere. And discussing him, apparently. Interesting. "Um, everything is fine, we're just leaving the Wheeler house now. And I have you on speakerphone in the car, by the way."

"What time is it... oh fu...dgesicles, it's after six already? How did it get so late?"

Zack chuckled at her near miss with the bad language. Hailey had filled them in earlier in the day about the swear jar in her grandmother's kitchen, and how it was going to fund her college education.

"Are you laughing at me, Zack Donovan? It's not funny, because we're still on the wrong side of the Sagamore Bridge and I left my car at Stephanie's house."

"It's all good. We were calling to ask if Hailey can sleep over at our house tonight."

"Please, Mom? It's not a school night," Hailey called from the back seat. "And I've slept over friend's houses before. And Bobby is my friend."

Erin was quiet for a long moment. "Can you take me off speakerphone, Zack?"

"No can do while I'm driving," he told her.

"Is this okay with you? Having a sleepover?"

"Hey, I'm the newbie at this parenting gig. You tell me. If you think it's a good idea, it's okay with me. They've already eaten pizza for dinner, and are pretty tired from playing outside most of the day."

"But we both want to stay up and watch the pirate movie, Mom. It's on tonight, we saw the ads while we were eating dinner. Mr. Z said if it's okay with you then I can stay."

"If you promise to listen to… Mr. Z, and be good, and go to sleep when he tells you, then I guess it's okay."

"We promise," both kids yelled.

"Thank you, Mrs. B," Bobby called as Hailey added, "Thanks, Mom."

Zack checked his rearview mirror, amazed that Karly stayed asleep throughout this entire exchange.

"Zack?" Erin's voice on the speaker sounded softer. "Thanks for doing this. I'll call you when I'm back on Cape."

"Don't worry about anything," Zack assured Erin. "I've got this under control. Go have fun, Ms. B."

"Okay thanks, Mr. Z." She disconnected, and the car speakers reverted to music.

Zack looked into the rearview mirror again to see Bobby and Hailey high five each other, as if they were embarking on an epic adventure together. "I didn't know you both liked pirates."

"We like all the same stuff, Uncle Z. It's so cool."

"Yeah, Mom always says if you find someone who likes the same things, that's who you want to be friends with," Hailey agreed.

"Sounds like your mom is pretty smart," Zack said, catching her eye in the rearview mirror.

"She really is," Hailey agreed without hesitation. "Bobby is lucky to have her as a teacher. I have Mrs. Wilson, one of Grandma's friends, so I can't say anything bad about her."

Zack stifled a grin. "Is she not a good teacher?"

Hailey sighed dramatically. "Not as good as Mom, that's for sure. She's old like Grandma, and has some old ideas. Like we're only allowed to color inside the lines."

Bobby nodded sagely, as if this was critical to the educational curriculum. "It's important to know how to do that, but it's also important to know when…"

"When a picture needs a background!" Hailey finished for him, and they smiled at each other.

"Exactly!" Bobby beamed.

Zack shook his head, but was smiling. Two kids obviously on the same page, so to speak.

CHAPTER 8

*E*rin hung up the phone and returned to the table of boisterous women who were in the process of ordering another pitcher of margaritas. Thanking the gods of alcohol that she wasn't one of the designated drivers in the group, she helped herself to another refill from the near-empty pitcher still on the table.

They'd driven off-Cape up to Wareham, where they shopped for hours and each found a fun outfit to wear to the "adult prom" as the women were calling it. Erin's find was a pale pink sheath with flirty ruffles at the bottom that dusted her knees and made her feel more daring than she had in years. Now they were having drinks and appetizers at Ruby something or other, one of the chain restaurants on the access road that led from the outlet mall to the highway.

Heavy wooden tables and chairs were offset by modern and colorful chandeliers hanging over the booths and tables. Mirrors covered the walls, and the large windows overflowed with masses of hanging plants. Table tents boasted seasonal pumpkin spice flavored cocktails, but the group had focused on the first page of the menu, which offered margaritas of every size, shape, and color. One of the sizes was "endless pitcher" and their group was taking full advantage.

The women commandeered three large tables and dragged them

closer together to accommodate their group. Erin hadn't hung out with most of these ladies since high school. Some of them not even then, since they'd all been in different social cliques. Now – as moms – it seemed they were all on more equal footing. She'd gotten to know – and actually like – a lot of them. Including the woman seated next to her.

"Everything okay at home?" Stephanie asked as Erin dropped back into her chair.

"All good. Remember I was just telling you that Zack took Hailey with them to Joe's?"

"And?"

"Zack called because the party wound down, and now Hailey wanted to ask if she could sleep over at Bobby's house."

"Oooo-oooh," chorused a few of the women seated nearby, followed by giggles. Endless margaritas at work.

"She's in kindergarten," Erin said with a laugh, waving off the extra attention. "Get your minds out of the gutter!"

More laughter followed her proclamation, but Stephanie still looked at her with a gleam in her eye. "Zack's nephew Bobby is Hailey's new BFF? So, you and Zack…"

"Are friends, like I told you the other day."

"Just friends?"

"Just friends," Erin said, trying to add a touch of steel to her tone. The look Stephanie gave her told Erin she hadn't done a good enough job of it. "Look, he's the guardian of one of my students. There can't be anything more than friendship."

The look on Stephanie's face turned assessing. "Is that school policy or your own personal preference?"

"I'm not sure," Erin answered, feeling flustered. "Both maybe? I know we're not supposed to date parents of students. It's a bad idea in general."

"Ah, but he's not a parent."

"Technically? No… but it's kind of the same thing." Erin needed a plausible excuse to keep him firmly in the friend zone. She wasn't about to admit her teenaged crush… or any of her more recent, and decidedly sexier, thoughts about the man.

Stephanie waved her hand between them. "We're friends now, right? I mean, after today and moving forward? I know I ignored you in high school, but you're a cool human being, Erin Brannigan."

"You're a cool human being too, Stephanie Ruhle. And that's not just the margaritas talking." They both laughed and bumped fists.

"Then let me give you some advice about Zack Donovan."

"I'm not sure…"

"Uh uh uh." Stephanie wagged a finger in front of her face. "You're gonna let me tell you a thing or two."

Erin leaned back in her chair. "Okay?"

Stephanie smiled at her. "Now, the thing about Zack is he's actually a nice guy. He might have himself a successful career that includes a hit TV show, but he's not stuck up about it. And yeah, he's probably been on People Magazine's short list for sexiest man on television, but he's still approachable."

"Okay?"

"He's been like that since high school. Down to earth. Easy to talk to. Well, you remember how he was back then, right?"

Erin asked the question she'd been avoiding since she'd seen them together on the soccer field sidelines. "Did you and Zack ever…"

The other woman shook her head. "Nope. I may have flirted with him here and there, but I knew even then that I wanted to stay on the Cape and raise a family. Zack was bound and determined to move to New York City. He liked growing up here well enough, but he wanted to see the world."

Erin could relate to that. Her own high school plans had been to dust the sand off her shoes after graduation and never return for longer than a holiday vacation. *And look how that plan turned out.*

"Anyway, there were plenty of guys, like my husband Jake, who planned to stick around and take over their family business. Zack was never one of them, so I didn't waste my time. But now I'm wondering if he plans to stick around this time? Or will he take the kids back to New York City with him?"

Erin frowned. After what Karly had told her, she'd tried to broach the subject with Zack. He insisted that he was committed to honoring his sister's wishes and being guardian to Bobby and Karly... but did he ever say he planned to stay? The thought of him moving with the kids hadn't occurred to her.

He did say he was still working on the spring season of *Epic Adventures*. He hadn't given up his television show. Was it possible he meant to leave the Cape again? And why did the thought twist her insides so much that it hurt?

She decided it might be safer to steer the subject away from Zack. Or at least away from the idea of him leaving Cape Cod any time soon.

Her mother's words from a month ago echoed in her head. *Isn't it time for the next adventure?*

Did she want Zack to be part of that adventure?

CHAPTER 9

Zack hit the pause button, freezing the video promo clip he'd been reviewing on his computer screen. He could've sworn he heard something. He listened again, but the house remained silent. *What was that noise? Is one of the kids awake?*

Karly had been in bed since they returned from Joe's house, totally worn out by the day. The older two changed into pajamas, pulling sleeping bags out of the closet and pillows off Bobby's bed before settling in front of the television to watch their pirate movie. He'd sat with them long enough to ascertain their choice of movie was age-appropriate, before removing himself to the dining room to get work done. He'd gone back in to shut off the television half an hour ago, both older kids fast asleep on the living room carpet, snuggled under a blanket fort.

He still didn't know what he was going to do about adding one more episode to the spring season, a dilemma he'd been worrying about while reviewing the promo teasers Mike forwarded.

Another sound, this time it was definitely coming from outside the house. Was that a car door slamming? Who would be in the driveway at this hour? *Oh shit, the doorbell will wake all the kids!*

Zack hurried to the door, socks sliding along the hardwood floor.

He yanked the door open in time to watch Erin stumble on the front porch stairs with shopping bags in one hand, the other grabbing onto the railing for balance. She looked at him and her face lit with a grin, her smile both innocent and filled with promises.

"Hi honey, I'm home," she said with a giggle that seemed out of character, before turning to wave at the car waiting in the driveway, engine still running.

Zack shifted his gaze to the SUV that was definitely not Erin's vehicle. He could see another woman's silhouette in the driver's seat but couldn't make out who it was as she backed out of the driveway and headed down the street. Leaving Erin here with him. He leaned against the open doorframe, arms crossing against his chest. "Are you... are you drunk?"

She giggled again and stepped up onto the porch to stand in front of him. "I knew you were a smart one. And yes. *Drunk* might be an adjective to describe my current state. Tipsy, wobbly, and buzzed may also apply. I may possibly, or probably, have had one too many margaritas from the endless pitcher. How can they afford to sell endless pitchers of margaritas anyway?"

He chuckled and ushered her into the house, her body brushing against him as she passed. "I'm sure I don't know. Was there food involved with these endless pitchers?"

She scrunched her nose. "Nachos. But, you know, I'm not a huge nacho fan. Or you probably don't know that, so I'm telling you. Nachos are messy, but not in a good way. Hard to eat." She looked at the jumble of shoes piled next to the door and toed off her own, kicking them toward the others and dropping the oversized shopping bags next to the pile.

He lifted one eyebrow and the bulging bags. "Successful day at the outlets?"

She made a face. "I'm so far behind on my Christmas shopping it isn't funny. I took advantage of being there and got my mom and Hailey some stuff too. But then the group decided happy hour should start early. And did I mention the endless margaritas?"

"Why don't we find you something to soak up some of that tequila?" He put a hand on the small of her back to steer her down the hallway to the kitchen. She leaned against into his side, and his hand slid to her hip, pulling her even closer. She fit next to him like a missing puzzle piece, her warm softness molding to his body like she belonged there.

"I didn't come here for you to feed me. In fact, I know I told Stephanie that I should go home because the kids were probably asleep and I didn't want to wake anyone by ringing the bell. But Sonya was driving and she listened to Stephanie and not to me. But you solved that problem, didn't you! So smart, like I said before."

Zack chuckled as he moved her to one of the stools at the kitchen island. "Are you always this chatty when you drink?"

She scrunched her nose again in thought, which Zack found oddly endearing. "I'm not sure the last time I had this much to drink. Or, you know, more than one drink in a night. It's been a while. Definitely since before Hailey was born."

"That long, huh?" He pulled some cheese and bread from the fridge, putting them on the counter next to the butter dish. Grilled cheese was fast and filling, and something he could easily make. And greasy food always tasted best when tipsy. Or late at night. It was one of his go-tos when he was working late and had to keep going.

She nodded, planting both elbows on the counter and resting her chin in her hands. "The whole single parent thing is tough. Always feeling like you need to have the answers, be in control, be ready for anything. Not a lot of time to let loose."

He nodded as he pulled out a frying pan and put together the sandwich. "I totally get that."

"Are you making me grilled cheese? How did you know that's one of my favorite late-night snacks?"

He shot her a look, trying to figure out if she was teasing him or not. "Isn't it everyone's favorite? But you know it's only nine, not actually all that late."

She giggled again, which was quickly becoming one of his favorite sounds. "When happy hour starts at three, it seems pretty late. And yes, I love grilled cheese. I hope you're making one for yourself, too. We can sit here and eat them together, right?"

"Sure." Actually, that sounded pretty good. He filled two glasses with water, putting one on the counter in front of Erin, before slapping cheese between two more slices of bread. He slid a chunk of butter in the pan to melt. "What else did you do with your Saturday, besides a lot of day drinking?"

While he tended the sandwiches in the pan, she regaled him with stories of dressing room laughter and everyone finding dresses for the "adult prom," and another about getting her chest measured at the Victoria's Secret outlet that he was positive she wouldn't have shared had she been sober.

"I told the salesgirl I'd been a B-cup all my life, but she proved me wrong and fitted me for a C-cup. Apparently, breastfeeding has that effect on lots of women. No wonder my bras have felt so constricting. I've been buying the wrong size! And you know, I thought lace underwear would be itchy, but it's really pretty comfortable."

Zack nearly choked on his water when she pulled her sweater down to one side to show off the very tippy top of the triangle of her apparently new lacy black bra in the correct cup size. Black lace straps over the creamy skin of her shoulder and clavicle, his imagination racing to fill in the rest... He put down the water glass and turned away to adjust himself, trying to hide his reaction.

He grabbed two dishes from the cabinet and plated the sandwiches, cutting each one into triangles. "Do you want mustard with this? Or potato chips?" he asked over his shoulder.

"Nah, just the cheesy goodness." She was smiling at him when he turned around to put the plate in front of her. "This smells delicious. Thank you."

"You're welcome." He brought his own plate and glass of water to the counter and sat on the stool at the end, the corner of the granite separating them, trying hard not to think about the black lace under her shirt.

He thought it would be difficult to carry on a normal conversation while sitting so close that their knees almost touched, being distracted with the way her lips wrapped so delicately around each small bite of her sandwich. But when she started asking questions about his travels, about specific episodes of his show, it was easy to answer, to joke with her, to talk about the highs and lows of the helicopter ski trip in the Canadian Rockies, or the time during Season One he tried his hand at bull riding during the Calgary Stampede and broke his arm. Luckily, they'd been at the end of filming for the season, and it made for a great finale episode. And got them renewed for another two seasons.

"I thought they'd cancel the show after that stunt, but instead the ratings went through the roof," he said, shaking his head at the memory. "Mike was ready to kill me for being so dumb as to think I could do something that takes years to master. He was overjoyed that the network included the footage of me at the hospital wearing that backless gown, which he definitely filmed as payback for my stupidity."

"Mike?" Erin tilted her head, popping the last bit of grilled cheese into her mouth.

"My cameraman. He's been with me since the beginning. Tall, bald, infectious grin?" Zack frowned. "I guess you wouldn't know him as he never actually appears on the show, he's always behind the camera, capturing the scenes."

"Are you two friends? Or just coworkers?"

Zack paused for a moment to consider her question. "You know, before Daphne died, I would've automatically said friends. No question. I would've even called him my best friend. We've spent so much time together over the last several seasons of filming, and we always get along great. We understand each other very well."

"Where has he been for the last few months?" Erin scrunched her nose, like she did when she talked about the messy nachos at the restaurant. As if the question itself offended her. "Not that I've been stalking you or anything, but it feels like I would've noticed if you'd had a friend hanging around Chatham. Or Bobby would've mentioned it in class during sharing time."

Zack laughed without humor. "That's why it took me a minute to think about it. He hasn't been to visit. Hasn't ever met Bobby and

Karly. Maybe I read more into our friendship than actually existed. To him, I'm just the show talent, the guy he needs to keep happy to keep his job. Not an actual friend."

Erin reached across the small space dividing them and laid her warm hand on top of Zack's. "Or maybe he's feeling unsure about what he can do to help you, given the situation. Have you talked to him since you moved back here last month?"

"Couple times a week at least. We're working on putting the spring season together to present to the network."

"Where is he now?"

"New York. At the studio for most of the past month, editing film. Since he's been with me the longest and he shot most of the footage, he's the expert on the team."

"And where would you normally be?"

"Sitting next to him. It's my show, after all."

She wrapped her hand around his, giving it a squeeze, her thumb sweeping slow circles against the back of his hand and sending warm tingles up his arm. "I think he's trying to help you the only way he knows how. Doing his job, and it sounds like he's trying to do yours as well."

Zack thought about it and shook his head. She had a point. "Maybe you're right. But some of it would be easier if he'd come to Chatham so we could collaborate in person."

"Did you invite him?"

A jolt of surprise ran through him. "No. I didn't think of it."

She shrugged. "Maybe you should." She tried to pull her hand back.

Before she could, Zack turned his so they were palm to palm, interlacing their fingers and giving her hand a squeeze. "You know, I still owe you an apology."

Her nose scrunched again, puzzlement clear in those ocean blue eyes. She looked so cute that he had to stop himself from kissing her. *She's not yours to kiss*, he reminded himself halfheartedly.

"Apologize for what?"

"For what I said that day at the church. At Daphne's funeral."

Her cheeks reddened and she looked away from him, trying again to pull her hand out of his.

He held firm, leaning across the corner that divided them and resting his forehead against hers. "I wasn't my best self that day... and it all started feeling so familiar, like my parents' funeral all over again."

"Zack, I..."

He cut her off, deciding to take a leap of faith. "When my parents died, everyone kept offering to help Daphne and me. But in the end, those were just words. Insurance money only went so far. After the first year, we had trouble paying bills. We relied on the food pantry for most of our food. It was rough until I graduated from high school and Daphne sold the house."

Her mouth fell open as he spoke, taking in his words. Her eyes searched his and must have believed whatever it was she saw there. "I... I had no idea you went through that back then."

"I didn't want anyone to know."

"But..."

He waved away her objections. "It was embarrassing enough to be known around town as the kid whose parents died in a plane crash."

"But... you graduated and went off-Cape for college."

"Loans and scholarships. I held a campus job all four years. Then I used my half of the house money to start my travel business after graduation. The right person saw my travel blog and videos and offered me a shot at a television show."

She nodded along with his words. "I remember my parents telling me about that. Big article about you in the Cape Cod Times, one of their students catching a break and making it big."

"I worked hard. I earned everything I have now." He closed his eyes and exhaled a long breath before continuing. "I don't want these kids to go through any of the same sort of hardships or choices Daphne and I faced. And standing in the church that day, I guess I got a little cynical about everyone's offers of help and support. Including yours."

Her eyes seemed softer, shimmering under the kitchen lights. "Oh Zack, I'm so sorry you went through that in high school. And I'm so sorry my words triggered you. If it helps any, I really meant them even when I said them. I want to be there, be here, for you and Bobby and Karly."

"I know that now." He leaned closer, their foreheads touching again. "Erin?"

"Yeah?" Her voice sounded breathy, like maybe she was thinking about the same thing he was.

"I'd really like to kiss you right now."

"I'd like that."

CHAPTER 10

Zack touched his lips softly to hers, a whisper of a kiss that sent a quick jolt all the way to his toes. Her sharp intake of breath against his mouth told him she felt the same electricity. Her lips parted and he took the invitation, his tongue licking along her bottom lip before plunging into her welcoming mouth, the kiss tasting of grilled cheese with a hint of tang from the margaritas she'd had earlier.

His hand rose to cradle the side of her face, holding it in place while he plundered her mouth, swallowing her low moan. Her hands gripped at the front of his shirt, as she rose from her stool. She spun his stool around so his back leaned against the counter and moved in closer, standing between his legs, her lips never breaking away from his.

Fireworks exploded behind his eyelids as the kiss deepened, each thrust of their tongues more hungry than the last. It felt like nothing he'd ever experienced, and at the same time it felt like coming home, the feeling of being exactly where he wanted to be.

Finally she broke away, panting for air. His lips chased hers for one last nibble.

"You taste even better than I ever imagined," she whispered.

Which made him smile and raise one eyebrow. He'd been thinking almost the exact same thing, but the thought of Erin fantasizing about him filled him with happiness. "How long have you been imagining my kisses, Erin Brannigan?"

The color on her cheeks deepened to match her well-kissed lips. "Longer than I'd care to admit."

"Are you kidding me? I feel like all you've been doing since I arrived in Chatham is giving me a hard time." He leaned in for another kiss, which turned into another hungry exploration.

This time he broke the kiss first, licking his lips. "So let me guess. You've been dreaming about me since the first season of *Epic Adventures*?" That's when the letters and emails had started pouring into Zack's office from women across the country.

Erin shook her head and giggled, suddenly sounding more shy than her bold kisses would have him believe.

"I crushed on you in middle school," she admitted. "You know, before we got to high school and you went all lax-bro-cool-dude."

He cupped her chin, running a thumb against those soft lips. "You didn't like jocks?"

She giggled again, her hands releasing the front of his shirt and sliding down to rest on the tops of his thighs. Her tongue darted out to lick her lips, brushing against his thumb and sending another surge of need through Zack. He sucked in a breath, his eyes locked with hers.

"You may recall the overwhelming power of high school cliques on the teenage mind. You were a jock, and I was an art nerd, and that kind of fraternization was frowned upon."

"And now?"

"Now it's fifteen years later and we're two consenting adults." She leaned in to kiss him again, her hands sliding up his thighs to brush where his dick strained against the zipper of his jeans, begging for release.

He sucked in another quick breath and pulled her hands away from the button at his waist. A flash of disappointment showed in her eyes, and he shook his head. "Erin, you've had a lot to drink today. You said it earlier, the endless margaritas kicked your ass."

"I still know what I want," she said stubbornly, leaning closer to lick his bottom lip. "And I want you. Now."

He closed his eyes as the rest of his blood rushed south, testing the limits of his restraint. "What I mean is, if this is really what you want, you'll still want it tomorrow. When you're sober enough to make a decision that's not margarita-flavored."

She stood there silent, her eyes searching his, as her wandering hand once again slid along his thigh, pressing against his rock-hard dick. "What about you? What do you want?"

Zack groaned. "I think you know what I want. To be inside you. To taste every part of your body with my tongue and make love to you all night long."

Long lashes blink rapidly over hungry, hungry blue eyes. "That sounds pretty good to me."

He removed her hand from his lap and pressed it to his chest, where she could feel his heart beating rapidly, and hopefully feel the honesty of his next words. "I want to take this slow, and make sure it's not the margaritas making your decisions. I like you, Erin. I'd like to see where this... this... this *thing* between us might lead."

"It could lead straight to your bedroom if you weren't trying to be a gentleman," she grumbled.

Zack's smile widened. "What was that now?"

"Nothing." A reluctant smile tugged at the corners of her luscious mouth. She sighed. "I guess I understand that you might have a teensy point about the endless pitcher thing."

He released her hands and she took a wobbly step away from him, steadying herself against the granite counter.

"I should probably..." She jerked a thumb over her shoulder, in the general direction of the front door.

"You don't have to leave," he argued gently. "Stay. Talk with me some more."

"Talk?" She smirked, batting her lashes at him in a way he found utterly adorable. "Is that what the cool kids are calling it these days?"

"I dunno, I've never actually been one of the cool kids," he countered, standing up and taking her hand. He laced their fingers together and pulled her toward the living room. "I just play one on TV."

"Oh, you're good, Zack Donovan," Erin said with a laugh. She stopped abruptly in the doorway, noticing the blanket fort for the first time, Hailey and Bobby sprawled in their sleeping bags, the television still playing some animated movie.

"Shoot, I forgot they were sleeping in here," Zack said, dropping her hand and skirting the edge of the room until he found the remote near Bobby's sleeping bag. He clicked the off button and turned back to see the soft smile on Erin's face as she took in the scene.

"Looks like they're getting along," she whispered.

"It was a good day," Zack agreed, matching her smile. "All around."

CHAPTER 11

*E*rin cracked one eyelid to see that dawn had indeed invaded her reality. She closed it again, trying to check in with the rest of her body. Her tongue felt like sandpaper as it tried to pry itself from the roof of her mouth. Why did her limbs feel imbued with concrete? And who let that woodpecker into her brain?

Oh right. Endless tequila.

The thought of margaritas made her stomach lurch in unsavory ways. *Not a thing that will happen again any time soon,* she promised herself before rolling onto her back. She carefully stretched her arms to the sides and her toes down toward the footboard, feeling the muscles stretch in protest. How was she so sore after a day of shopping? Hangovers felt a whole lot different at thirty-three than they had back in her twenties.

She opened both eyes to half mast, watching the ceiling fan turn in slow lazy circles.

A jolt zipped through her body and her eyes flew wide.

Ceiling fan?

Her bedroom didn't have a fan in it. In fact, her house didn't have *any* ceiling fans in *any* of the rooms.

What. The. Hell?

Where am I?

She bolted upright and immediately regretted the sudden movement, closing her eyes and pressing a palm to her forehead, mostly to keep her brain from exploding. When the pounding slowed, she opened them again and took a careful look around the room.

Walls of the palest shade of blue, the offsetting trim a brilliant white. Matching twin side tables in a light oak with candlestick lamps flanked the queen-sized bed where she currently sat. A pile of books on the left table, a square vase filled with sea glass on the one closer to her, where her cell phone sat plugged into a wall outlet. Four framed prints of alternating mountain and beach views lined the wall behind the bed. A long dresser stood against the far wall, with a mirror and an oversized flat screen hanging next to each other. Gauzy white curtains covered the windows, not doing enough to block the offending sunshine. A white door stood partway open, showing a closet full of neatly hung clothes.

Men's clothes.

And just like that, what happened after the endless pitchers of margaritas came rushing back.

Laughing with the other women in the SUV as Sonya Hamilton drove over the Bourne Bridge.

Getting dropped off at Zack's house instead of her own.

Zack making grilled cheese in his kitchen.

Talking about his wild travels and adventures.

Zack kissing her.

Zack kissing her.

Oh my god, Zack kissed her! And she kissed him right back!

She melted back onto the mattress and buried her head under the fluffy white pillow, letting out a quiet growl of frustration. *Stupid tequila!* But then again...now that she remembered, she knew kissing Zack had been better than she'd dreamed – and she'd dreamed of them plenty back in the day – soft and sweet and hard and hungry... and then... and then...

She couldn't remember anything after the kissing-in-the-kitchen portion of the evening.

What had she done?

Panicking only a little, she threw off the pillow and did a quick body scan. While her feet were bare, she still had on the same jeans and shirt she'd worn all day shopping. Yes, she was in bed and under the covers, but with all her clothes on. Including that new black lace underwear set Stephanie had talked her into buying and wearing out of the store. Okay, so maybe there wasn't anything after the kissing portion of the evening. So why was she sleeping in a bed that wasn't hers?

And why was the house so dang quiet?

Huffing out a breath, she slowly sat up. The woodpecker rat-a-tatting on the top of her head seemed to have slowed his pace, at least enough that it didn't feel like her brain might start oozing out of her ear bit by bit. *No more margaritas. Ever.*

Gingerly she put her feet on the hard wood floor and stood. *So far so good*, she thought. Opening the door to the hallway, she heard her daughter's voice drifting up the stairs.

"Can you make the next batch look like sailboats? Mom always makes her pancakes into fun shapes on Sunday mornings."

Right. Hailey's sleepover with Bobby. That's why she'd come to Zack's house last night instead of going home. Except all the kids had already been asleep by the time she got to the house. And Zack had teased her about being tipsy. Made her grilled cheese. Kissed the living daylights out of her. Her fingers gently touched her lips, running along the bottom one as she remembered the feel of his mouth on hers. Closing her eyes, she took a steadying breath. When she opened them again, Karly stood in front of her wearing purple pajamas with flying unicorns all over them, a serious look on her face.

Erin cleared her throat. "Good morning, Karly. Love your pjs."

"Thanks. Grandma bought them for me because girls are supposed to like unicorns. I like the ones with the poop emojis better. Uncle Z gave me those last Christmas but they're too small now."

Erin battled a smile as she tried to match the little girl's serious tone. "I completely understand."

"Are you here for pancakes?"

"Yes I am." Erin knew the simplest answer was usually best with young children.

Karly nodded, as if everything about this was perfectly normal. "Mommy used to make pancakes every Sunday after church. Uncle Z doesn't take us to church, but he's getting much better at Sunday pancakes. Even if he still burns the bacon most of the time. Are you good at bacon?"

Her heart stuttered painfully at the reminder that these kids had lost both parents just weeks before. "I'm sure your uncle will get better with some practice, just like he did with the pancakes."

The girl huffed out a breath. "Maybe," she said in a cynical tone that sounded much older. "But everyone needs help sometimes. Mommy always says Uncle Z doesn't like to ask for help."

"Then maybe we should go help him, whether he asks us or not." Erin offered her hand to the girl.

Karly wrapped her fingers around Erin's and tugged her toward the stairs. "Good idea."

In the kitchen, they found Hailey and Bobby standing on chairs against a counter covered in flour, wet drips of batter speckling their faces. Zack bent over in front of the refrigerator, rummaging through one of the bottom drawers. On the stovetop, bacon sizzled in a large cast iron frying pan.

"Uh oh, he's already burning it," Karly said quietly, rolling her eyes.

Hailey turned, her eyes lighting when she spotted them in the doorway. "Mom! Are you here for breakfast?"

"We're making Sunday pancakes, Mrs. B," Bobby added, gesturing at an electric griddle on the counter that Erin hadn't noticed.

"That sounds great," Erin said warily, releasing Karly's hand and stepping closer to flip the switch for the vent over the stovetop. Grabbing the nearby tongs she turned the bacon over, noting that a few of the slices already looked extra crispy. "Who's in charge of the bacon?"

"Oh fu— fudgesicles," Zack said, straightening as he shut the fridge door, a box of blueberries in his hand. "I was looking for the berries and forgot."

"We needed them to make smiley faces," Hailey explained. "Can you believe they don't have chocolate chips? I mean, who doesn't have chips in the house? How can they make chocolate chip cookies?"

Erin stifled a smile and pushed the bacon around in the pan. "Is there a bowl to spoon out some of this bacon fat?"

She felt the heat from Zack's body as he came closer and placed a ramekin next to the stovetop. "Here, I can cook the bacon," he said, his breath warming the back of her neck as he spoke, his hand coming to rest on her hip and trying to nudge her aside.

"Happy to help," she told him, planting her feet more squarely so as not to be moved. She turned her head slightly to meet his eyes. They were moonstone grey this morning, and swirling with questions. For some reason, seeing his uncertainty boosted her confidence. "Besides, your niece tells me you tend to overcook the bacon."

Zack shot Karly a mock scowl. "Traitor."

The girl shrugged and boosted herself onto one of the island stools. "I tell it like I see it, Uncle Z."

"Your bacon is very crispy," Bobby added diplomatically.

"I guess we'll see if Ms. Brannigan can do any better." Zack huffed as if he were seriously put out, but when she turned her head to check on his reaction he winked.

Trying hard not to laugh out loud at the back and forth between the kids and Zack, Erin focused her attention to the bacon sizzling in the pan. He was still standing a little too close, close enough that if she leaned back just a bit she'd end up nestled against that hard, muscled chest, the one she could remember running her hands up and down the night before. Here, in this kitchen. She felt the blush heating her cheeks as she remembered the feel of him under her hands… her body suddenly went stiff as she remembered wanting to take it further than kisses. And him shutting her down.

He must have noticed the change in her posture. "Hey, what's wrong?" he rumbled in her ear, his barely-there words too soft for the kids to hear over their continued banter about what constituted the right amount of crispiness for bacon. His hands settled on her hips, sending warm shock waves to her core. "Didn't you sleep well?"

"I got plenty of sleep, thank you," she said primly. *In that big bed, all alone, by myself*, she added in her head, flipping the meat in the pan one last time.

"You fell asleep before the deli scene, so I figured you needed sleep more than *When Harry Met Sally*," he said in his normal voice.

"Mom loves that movie! She fell asleep watching TV? I thought she drove over this morning?" Hailey was staring at her mother now. Her daughter with the ultrasonic hearing, except when it was something she didn't feel like doing.

Erin opened her mouth to answer, but her mind totally blanked. Zack rescued her.

"She came over to check on you last night, but you two pirates fell asleep on the living room floor right after your movie, so we went to the guest room to watch something else," he told her. "Your mom must've been tired from shopping all day and fell asleep, so I let her stay there."

Hailey snorted a laugh. "Yeah, she hates shopping."

"Me too," agreed Bobby. "Except for the duck store."

"I love that place!" Hailey and Karly said in unison.

"The what now?" Zack turned his confused eyes from one person to the next. "You mean the garden center at the edge of town?"

Erin shook her head and laughed. "I'm guessing the kids mean the rubber duck store on Main Street."

Zack focused on her and raised an eyebrow.

She raised one of her own. *Two can play at this game.* "You've never been to the duck store?"

"I've never even heard of such a place," he admitted, taking another step away from her, arms crossing over his chest. "I need details."

"It's awesome, Uncle Z," Bobby said, happy to provide those details. "All they have in the whole store is rubber ducks. Big ones, little ones, plain ones, fancy ones, and ducks dressed up for different holidays. You have to see it to believe it!"

Zack nodded, his eyes sparkling as they held Erin's gaze. "I think a field trip may be required."

She nodded, happy the direction of the conversation shifted.

He leaned closer to whisper in her ear, hot breath sending a shiver down her spine. "And then I think we need to talk."

CHAPTER 12

"I can't believe that store can stay in business when all they sell is rubber duckies. All those little happy plastic faces creeped me out." Zack pretended to shudder with horror.

"And yet you still bought up half the store," Erin said, nodding to the bag on the bench next to him. After the duck store, the kids had dragged them into a nearby bookstore. And then insisted on a trip into the chocolate shop in time to watch through the windows as the candy bakers in the back room made a batch of handmade candy canes for the upcoming holiday season, explaining each step of the process for the gathered crowd.

Then Zack proceeded to buy every flavor of candy cane in the store.

Zack shrugged and shifted his gaze over to the arcade games in the back of the pizzeria where they'd stopped in to have lunch. All three kids were laughing and arguing at the same time, like everything was normal in their lives, and he felt his heart squeeze tightly. "I'll do anything to make them smile like that any time I can," he said, trying to get a handle on the sudden surge of emotion. "Besides, I think my crew in New York will get a kick out of the adventure set I bought for them, don't you?"

"Who wouldn't love little scuba gear ducks, skiing ducks, and mountain climbing ducks?" Erin grinned and rolled her eyes. "Now, if only they'd had one with a parachute or being eaten by a shark…"

"Hey," he protested with a laugh. "I've never lost anyone on any of my adventures. Not even to a hungry shark. Although we came close on our last trip."

She sat up and stared at him. "Really? What happened?"

"I thought one of the guys had a heart attack in the shark cage," Zack told her, remembering the panic he felt when he's seen Chuck slumped to the cage floor. "Turns out he fainted when the Great White got too close to us." He omitted the part where he'd stuck his arm out of the cage to pet the impressive monster shark, causing the guy to faint in the first place.

Erin searched his face for a moment before focusing her gaze somewhere past him, toward the bar area of the restaurant before she asked her next question. "Do you miss it? The adrenaline rush?"

The question surprised him, if only because it wasn't the question he expected from her. Or what he wanted to talk about with her right this minute, quite honestly. He wanted to ask her about the confession she'd made in his kitchen the night before. Wanted to ask her what she felt… if she wanted… for fuck's sake, if he couldn't get the question right in his head, how could he ask her anything? And she had yet to mention last night. At all. Not a word.

Maybe she was embarrassed that she'd said too much, talking about old crushes and whatnot.

Or worse, maybe she was embarrassed that she'd kissed him.

His gaze focused on her wide, full lips, reliving the kiss they'd shared.

"Zack?"

His eyes darted away from those siren lips and met her knowing gaze. "What was the question again?"

A small smile tugged her lips, as if she could read his mind and knew where it had wandered. "Do you miss traveling?"

He shrugged. "I guess? Honestly, I feel like I've been running too hard keeping up with everything to miss it. Taking care of the kids is a full-time job, like an *epic adventure* all on its own."

"It certainly can be."

"About last night…"

Erin covered her face with both hands. "I'm sorry. I shouldn't have shown up on your doorstep drunk."

"Hey now." He pulled one hand away from her eyes and held it with both hands. "I'm glad you did."

"Really?"

"Really. If I didn't make it obvious last night, I kind of like you, Erin Brannigan."

She huffed out a laugh, her other hand finally falling to the scarred wooden table. "Right. You like me so much that I woke up alone, fully clothed, in your guest room."

Zack grinned. "You fell asleep on me watching a movie. In my bed."

"In your…" her voice trailed off. "Where did you sleep?"

"With you curled up next to me."

"But…"

He shook his head. "Nothing happened because you'd had one too many *endless* margaritas at the outlet mall. And you woke alone in bed because Bobby and Hailey got up early, demanding pancakes."

"Okay…"

"Erin. I like you. I want to explore whatever this thing is between us, maybe take you out on a date. You know, to a restaurant."

"This is a restaurant. We ordered food and everything."

He lifted an eyebrow. "You know what I mean. A *real* date."

She huffed out a laugh, gesturing around the pizzeria. "You mean this isn't real enough?"

He glanced over to the arcade area again, where the kids still seemed enthralled with the game they played. "Maybe without three kids tagging along?"

She smiled again and cocked her head to the side. "Zack. This is the reality of being a single parent. It's a package deal."

Before he could protest, the server arrived with a tray laden with two enormous pizzas, an order of mozzarella sticks, and enough French fries to feed a small army. As she unloaded the plates onto the table, the kids scrambled into their seats and immediately started arguing about whether the shaker of parmesan was the "right" kind of cheese. He caught Erin trying to hide her smile while the two older kids quickly got into a fry measuring contest in search of the longest ones in the basket, bickering like siblings and trying to enlist Erin to judge.

She was right. This was his new reality.

And he didn't mind one bit.

CHAPTER 13

Thanksgiving

*E*rin glanced yet again at the clock on the kitchen wall while she half-listened to a few of her cousins argue about whether the Patriots would make it to the Superbowl in February. Maureen and two of her sisters-in-law were laughing as they cut up green beans and tossed together a huge salad, the delicious smell of roasting turkey permeating the air.

Zack and the kids should arrive soon. The thought made her both nervous and excited, for reasons she shouldn't think too much about, not with her entire family surrounding her.

Oh. My. God. She was about to introduce the star of her recurring fantasies to her entire family. Introduce him as... what exactly? Certainly not her boyfriend. They hadn't even been on a date yet that didn't include small children tagging along.

It was one thing to invite Zack and the kids to a family dinner.

It was another thing entirely when thirty people were involved. And had opinions.

While she'd been an only child growing up, Erin enjoyed the benefits of being part of a large family. Both of her father's younger brothers were married with three kids each, all the cousins younger than Erin. Her mom was the youngest of three, that aunt and uncle both married with two kids each, all four of them older than Erin and married with more kids of their own. Altogether, four aunts, four uncles, ten first cousins, a few spouses, and another six second cousins. More than a houseful when they all gathered together.

Although they saw each other often throughout the year, especially the families that lived on the Cape year-round, Thanksgiving and Fourth of July were the two times every year that the entire clan made the effort to always be all together. While overwhelming at times, it made both holidays all the more joyous.

"Erin, honey, can you take more snacks out to the crowd in the living room?"

Her mother's voice cut through Erin's thoughts. She was still a teensy bit angry with the woman for inviting Leo for the holidays, but today wasn't the day for grudges. Thanksgiving was a day for family and being thankful for their love and support. Even when they annoyed her. "Sure, Mom."

She found more chips and pretzels in the pantry, poured them into bowls, and carried them to the family room for the crowd watching college football with her father. His younger brothers from Ohio and New Jersey had arrived the night before with their wives and families, and those living on Cape made it in time for the annual pancake breakfast at the Chatham Community Center. A large group left from there to attend the local high school football game, but should be returning to the house shortly. Hailey was in heaven playing with the crowd in the backyard, where lively games of cornhole and spike ball were being argued over.

Zack and the kids should arrive any minute, and the anticipation was making her stomach flutter in strange ways. It had been three full days since she'd seen him or spoken with him. Or kissed him.

Too long.

After lunch downtown on Sunday, he'd dropped her and Hailey at

Stephanie's house to pick up Erin's car. And accepted her invitation to spend Thanksgiving dinner with the Brannigan clan, instead of attempting to cook a turkey on his own.

Maureen happily added another place setting at the dining room table, and an additional two at the kids' table in the kitchen. Hailey was thrilled to have the chance to introduce everyone to her new best friend Bobby. And Erin had been ducking questions from well-meaning aunts and cousins all morning about her new "friend."

"Are you dating or just friends?"

"The actual Zack Donovan from television? Or someone else with that name?"

"Did you really go to high school with him?"

"Is Zack as hot in real life as he looks on TV?"

"Are those arm muscles real or photoshopped?"

"Does he kiss well?" Her cousin Sophie always got right to the point.

She'd tried her best to deflect their nosy inquiries, mostly because she wasn't quite sure where she stood with him. Yes, he told her that he liked her and wanted to try dating, and yes, he kissed like an absolute god, but she wasn't about to admit either of those things to her cousins. Especially after the radio silence for the better part of a week. Just a single text exchange earlier that morning to confirm what time he should arrive with the kids, and what they should bring.

Knowing that grilled cheese and frozen pizza were the limit of Zack's culinary skills, she suggested he bring beer and soda. To which he responded with a thumbs up emoji instead of actual words.

If he was really interested, shouldn't he have acted like it? Called? Texted? Stopped by?

Granted, she'd been busy at school getting Thanksgiving centerpiece projects finished to go home on Wednesday, and busy at home helping her mom prepare for the holiday. Food shopping, polishing the silverware, getting out Maureen's good china, decorating the house, baking enough pies so that everyone would have their favorite...

Giving her plenty of time to overthink every last conversation she and Zack shared. And whether he'd been sincere about wanting to go on what he referred to as a "real date."

A shiver ran through her at the thought.

If nothing else, he would be her date to the reunion prom on Saturday. Two days away. Maureen and Tom agreed to babysit all three kids that night for a sleepover. Despite her anxiety over the radio silence, Erin was hoping to have a sleepover of her own. In Zack's bed. This time, without her clothes. And without his clothes. She wanted to lick that shark tattooed on his shoulder, and trail her fingers along the hard planes of his abs...

Another delicious shiver ran through her body.

Hailey came in the backdoor with her usual whirlwind of energy. "Mom! Is Bobby here yet? We're picking teams to have a scavenger hunt. And Grandma, we need some lunch bags to gather stuff."

"What kind of scavenger hunt?" Erin turned to Maureen. "Mom? Did you plan something for the cousins?"

Aunt CeCe raised her hand. "We brought it from home. It's a foliage hunt the kids did at school this week when I was the classroom helper. They gather leaves of different colors and shapes, acorns, stuff like that. I made extra copies of the sheets, figuring the trees on Cape Cod aren't that different than the ones in New Jersey."

"That sounds wonderful, CeCe." Maureen beamed at her sister-in-law, raising her wine glass to toast her. "You'll have to show me a copy later."

"I'll get the bags for you," Erin told Hailey as she went to the pantry. "But you might have to start without Bobby since he's not here yet."

"But Mo-o-om," Hailey started to whine, just as the doorbell chimed. Her face broke out into a giant smile. "I'll bet that's him!" She raced out of the kitchen toward the front door.

Part of Erin wanted to follow in her daughter's wake and run to greet their guests, her heart skipping a beat in anticipation of seeing Zack. Instead, she ducked into the pantry and pulled out a handful of brown paper bags for the cousins to gather foliage and acorns and took them out into the backyard where her cousin Blake, CeCe's oldest and as tall as Erin at only sixteen, seemed to be in charge of distributing the checklists and markers to the teams.

"Thanks," he told her, taking the bags. He swept shaggy blond hair off his damp forehead, his wide grin making him look more like a kid than a teenager. "Did you want to get in on the hunt? We're dividing the teams now."

"Not me, but Hailey's friend just got here and they need to be on a team."

Blake nodded. "They're with me. Don't worry, I'll keep an eye on them."

Hailey burst through the back door, dragging Bobby by the hand. "We're here! We're here! We can start the treasure hunt now!"

"Treasure?" Erin looked to Blake for clarification.

He shrugged. "Whatever works, right?"

Grinning, she gave Hailey and Bobby each a pat on the head. "You two be good and listen to Blake's instructions, okay? He's your team leader. And don't go too far from the house. We'll be sitting down to eat in an hour."

Bobby smiled up at her. "Uncle Z told me to say thank you for inviting us as soon as I saw you. Today is already so much better than Thanksgiving used to be!"

"And why's that?"

Bobby wrinkled his nose, as if the memories smelled bad. "We always flew to Florida to be with my grandparents and stay in their smelly house. And there was only pumpkin pie for dessert, even though Mommy and I both hate it. Grandma said it was tradition. And all Grandpa does is watch football. He never plays with us."

"Oh, Bobby..."

The boy shrugged. "It's okay. Mom always tried to make it fun. And we talked to Grandma today so she's not lonely without us. She and Grandpa are coming to visit at Christmas."

Even as Erin's heart broke a little, Hailey put an arm around her friend. "Don't worry. My aunt made pumpkin pie, but we also have twelve other desserts. I'll bet you'll like one of them."

"Thirteen desserts?" Bobby's eyes were wide and eager.

Hailey nodded solemnly. "Every year. It's the luckiest number, *my* grandma says."

"Is one of the desserts your famous chocolate chip cookies?"

"Of course I baked cookies," Hailey told him. "But they don't count as one of the desserts. They're just a snack. But I helped Mom with some of the real desserts too."

Bobby bounced on his toes. "I can't wait! Best Thanksgiving ever!"

Clearing the emotion from her throat, Erin smiled brightly and tipped her head toward Blake. "Listen to your team captain and have fun, you two."

CHAPTER 14

Zack stood at the back of the large family room, chatting with his high school history teacher, Mr. Brannigan – *Call me Tom* – and his brother Brad, who lived in New Jersey and taught at Rutgers University. Apparently, the desire to teach ran in the family.

"Thanks again for inviting me and the kids for Thanksgiving, Tom. And for inviting Aunt Dolores too, although she sends her regrets." Zack shook his head. "Apparently she hosts a Thanksgiving feast for all the single octogenarians in Wellfleet, or something like that."

The older man frowned. "I thought she was your only family in the area?"

"That's right." Heat creeped up Zack's neck, remembering all the times during his teens when he and Daphne needed the help of family. Help that never came.

He'd heard from his great aunt exactly twice since Daphne's funeral. Once before Columbus Day to ask if he and the kids were going to visit Wellfleet for the town-wide oyster festival (which the kids had no interest in attending), and again last week to let him know she couldn't possibly join them for Thanksgiving. She told him she would try to visit for Christmas.

Tom cleared his throat. "Well, we're happy to have you here. And

Hailey is thrilled to have Bobby here. Those two have really hit it off. She'll miss him when you all move."

It was Zack's turn to frown. "Move? We're not planning to move anywhere."

"Oh. But I assumed... What about your show?"

"Yeah, will there be another season of *Epic Adventures*?" Brad asked, sipping his beer like the question wasn't a bomb waiting to explode.

"We have episodes ready to air for next spring's season," Zack told him, keeping to the simple truth. "After that, I'm not sure what we're going to do. Things have...changed."

Tom explained to his brother, "Zack's sister passed away in September and he was named guardian of his niece and nephew. Speaking of whom, where are those kids?"

Grateful for the change of subject, Zack hooked a thumb over his shoulder toward the back of the house. "Hailey grabbed Bobby and ran off as soon as we arrived, and your wife took Karly into the kitchen to get a snack."

And to wash the last of the syrupy stickiness from the girl's face, leftover from the pancake breakfast at the Community Center. The stickiness Zack hadn't noticed and Karly hadn't mentioned until Mrs. Brannigan – *Please call me Maureen* – opened the front door.

"Hard to travel the world with little kids in tow," Brad said, sipping his beer. "Totally understand that one. We watch your show as a family, and Blake's been begging for a while now to go to the Calgary Stampede, but we figured it would be more fun for everyone once the kids were a little older."

Zack nodded in agreement. "I guess most of my adventures aren't really family-friendly trips."

"The helicopter skiing last winter? Breathtaking to watch you guys leap out onto the snowy mountain, but definitely not something I want the wife and kids to try anytime soon. All the same, great to watch and live vicariously. Do you think spring be the last season of *Epic Adventures* then?"

"As I said, I'm not sure what's going to happen," Zack said, shifting uncomfortably. He didn't want to talk about the future right now, not when he wasn't sure what he was going to do. He and Mike had hard discussions every day this week, trying to figure out not only the final episode for this season, but a path forward for the show in general. "The network might find a new host, or the show might be over... We're still in discussions as to what happens next fall."

"Well, I for one hope you figure out a way to make it work," Brad said, tipping his beer bottle toward Zack. "You're the heart of the show."

"Appreciate that."

"Zack! There you are! I was starting to think Bobby and Karly came over without you."

Erin stood in the same hallway where Maureen and Karly disappeared minutes before, the sight taking his breath away. Her blond hair was pulled back in a low bun, a few loose wisps framing her heart shaped face, with a smile so bright it lit up the entire room. A silky red blouse and tight denim jeans covered all those curves that had haunted his dreams for weeks now. A white bibbed apron tied around her waist. Drawings of wine glasses filled with red, white, and pink liquids ran across the top, with the words *My doctor says I need glasses.*

Swallowing down the sudden urge to grab on and hold her tight, he lifted the twelve pack of Sam Adams he'd picked up at the liquor store. "You told me to bring beer, but your apron says you prefer wine?"

Mr. Brannigan – *Tom* – laughed. "Oh no worries on that account. One of my brothers-in-law is in the wine business, and insists on bringing enough bottles every Thanksgiving that they last us through New Year's Eve."

Erin looked down at her apron and shook her head, her hands going to the back and untying the strings. "I forgot I had this on. My aunt gifted it to me last Christmas. Let's drop those beers in the cooler and I'll make some quick introductions."

Quick introductions lasted quite a while. Aunts in the kitchen giving him hugs, uncles and cousins turning away from the football game to stand and shake his hand, a few who asked for behind the scenes gossip about his show, and then another horde of family members returned from the high school football game and it seemed like the introductions started all over again.

Almost every single one had questions about one or another of his televised adventures, similar to the fan meet-and-greets his publicity team set up at the start of each new season. The difference now was that Erin stayed by his side the entire time, carrying Karly on her hip and shutting down the cousins who asked personal questions with a quick retort and redirect. Better than any PR pro he'd ever worked with. *Definitely need to drag her along on the next publicity tour.*

The thought stopped him in his tracks for a minute. Bring her to New York for the promo tour? That implied something more... well, something *more* between them than several heated arguments, sharing a few meals together with their kids, and one heavy duty make-out session. They hadn't even gone on a real date yet. Or gotten naked together. Yet.

But when he looked at her, he could taste those kisses on his tongue.

And he wanted more.

Finally, after meeting half a million members of the extended Brannigan clan, Zack realized he hadn't seen Bobby or Hailey since his arrival. "Where are the kids?"

Erin gestured toward the back of the house. "The younger cousins are all doing a scavenger hunt. Bobby arrived just in time to join the fun."

"Wait, there are more cousins?"

She laughed. "You haven't met the sixteen-and-under crowd yet. My dad's the oldest of three, their kids are younger than us, and my mom's the youngest of three, so her niece and nephew have kids of their own."

Karly spoke up. "That's why there are thirteen pies on the kitchen table, waiting for dessert time."

Zack's eyes ping ponged between Karly and Erin. "Thirteen pies?"

Erin nodded, her smile wide. "Well, twelve flavors of pies and Aunt Barbara's famous chocolate Bundt cake. And ice cream. And home-made whipped cream. Oh, and a box of chocolate truffles Sophie brought from the shop she works at."

Karly patted Erin's cheek to get her attention. "Does she work at the place we watched them making candy canes?"

"No, sweetie. She lives in Ohio and works at a chocolate shop there."

"Can we visit her and watch her make chocolate?"

Erin's eyes connected with Zack before answering. "Ohio is pretty far away from Cape Cod."

"Uncle Z likes to travel. He can take us there. It can be one of his adventures.

Zack shifted closer and plucked Karly from Erin's arms and gave her a hug. "I'm here with you and Bobby now. No more adventures for a while."

"Why not?" she asks, only curiosity in her voice and none of the censure he'd heard from Mike and others on the same topic.

"Because we're a family now, and family sticks together at home," he tried to explain.

"But I want to go to adventuring." The stubborn look on the girl's face told him she wasn't convinced by his argument. In fact, the look on her face told Zack they were on the verge of an epic tantrum. But why? Telling her he was staying right here by her side should make the kid happy, shouldn't it?

He'd changed his plans, his life, his everything for Karly and her brother. What more could he do?

Luckily, Erin intervened and changed the focus. "Speaking of adventuring, let's go see how the scavenger hunt is going, shall we? Come this way," she said, making exaggerated motions with both arms, as if directing traffic.

Karly giggled, and the impending tantrum dissolved like a puff of smoke. As if a backyard adventure was just as exciting as a trip to Ohio or swimming with sharks. Maybe to a three-year-old they were all equivalent.

The thought circled his mind like leopard sharks around fresh meat. He felt like there was more to the idea, but just slightly out of reach. Maybe…

"Uncle Z! Uncle Z!" Bobby ran up and threw his arms around Zack's legs the moment he stepped off the back deck and onto the lawn. "Hailey has a gazillion cousins and I made a ton of new friends and my team won the treasure hunt! This is the best day ever!"

"That's awesome, buddy. Glad you're having fun." Zack lowered a squirming Karly to the ground so she could run to greet Hailey on the far side of the lawn. "Can I assume you've been behaving yourself like we talked about and not causing any trouble?"

Bobby nodded, puffing out his chest. "I sure did. I'm the best guest ever. Blake even said so. He was my team captain and even though he's sixteen he said we're friends now."

A lanky blond teenager came up behind Bobby, pushing hair out of his eyes. "Mr. Donovan? It's so awesome to meet you in person. I watch your show every week. Even the reruns. The stuff you do is amazing!"

"Uncle Z, this is Blake Brannigan," Bobby said, gesturing to the taller boy. "My new friend."

Zack nodded. Of course a teenager would befriend his nephew to get closer to a television star. He'd probably pull out a phone any second and ask for a selfie for social media.

The kids were going to have to get used to being fame-adjacent, as it were, and understand not everyone was really their friends. He gave the teen the same smile he'd been using inside, polite and practiced. "Nice to meet you, Blake. Your dad says you want to visit Canada for the Calgary Stampede someday. To compete or just watch?"

"Oh, totally just to watch, to be there in person. That's my favorite episode of all time. And the way you got in there and rode that bull was freaking awesome! I mean, you're not a cowboy but you did it anyway! And broke your arm, but the way you just went for it without fear was just… awesome."

Bobby's chest was puffed up again. "I told you. My Uncle Z is awesome. He's like a real-life super hero, but without the fancy gadgets."

The older boy ruffled Bobby's hair. "You were awesome today too, kid. Sorry I didn't believe you when you said that your uncle is *the* Zack Donovan. I mean, we don't get many TV stars coming to Thanksgiving dinner."

"Don't go inflating this guy's ego, Blake." Erin bumped her hip into Zack's. "He's already heard it all from the rest of the family. If his head gets any bigger, he won't fit in the dining room with the rest of us mere mortals."

Zack stared at the blond teen, watching him give Erin a quick hug before pulling Bobby back into the crowd gathering to play some other game. Had he really not known Bobby was related to him? And the sixteen-year-old still treated a six-year-old like a friend? He took a quick glance around the yard at the other groups of kids, noting that none of them were sneaking photos or even paying him much attention. Did his reality star status really not matter to any of them?

He felt his shoulders relax, not realizing how much tension he'd been holding until it started to dissipate.

A soft hand touched his arm. "Hey. Everything okay with you?"

His eyes connected with Erin's. "I'm fine."

"I know my family can be... a lot. And that there's too many of them. We don't all get together very often, but when we do, well, it can be overwhelming."

He couldn't help the small smile tipping his lips. "Maybe a little."

"It's okay. I understand if you want to sneak out the back gate. I'll drop the kids off at your house after they eat."

"What? Your family isn't so bad. I'm just not used to... well, I'm not used to people treating me like... like family instead of like a celebrity. And I mean that in the best possible way." He squeezed her hand to reassure her of the truth in his words. "Besides, there's no way I'm going to miss out on a turkey dinner."

"Don't forget the thirteen desserts," she reminded him, her smile once again wide. "It makes the chaos all worth the effort. I promise."

"I'm definitely looking forward to dessert," Zack said, taking her hand and twining their fingers together. "Even more than that, I'm looking forward to our date Saturday night."

"You mean the prom thing?" Her brows knit together in adorable confusion.

He nodded and used his free hand to gently smooth the furrow between her eyebrows. "Yeah, I mean the prom thing. You're my date for the evening, and I expect to dance with you all night."

"Aren't you going to want to catch up with your old friends? Dance with old girlfriends?"

"I didn't have any girlfriends in high school."

Erin scoffed. "Yes, you did. You took Cheryl Mapleton to Homecoming our junior year, and you brought Lila Nickerson to the senior prom."

"Those were dates. Not girlfriends." Zack shoved both hands in his pockets. "How could I have a girlfriend when I was embarrassed to bring anyone to our house? I didn't want them to see how empty the place was, after we sold most of the furniture to keep the heat on one winter. I didn't want anyone to know we were regular customers at the food pantry."

Her mouth fell open. "I had no idea."

"No one did."

"But..."

He shook his head, feeling like he needed to share this, make her understand how lucky she was to have this chaos of family togetherness at Thanksgiving. "Our family wasn't – isn't – like yours. Both sets of my grandparents died when I was two so I don't remember any of them. My parents were both only children. My grandfather's sister still lives in Wellfleet, but she's... eccentric. Not someone to rely on."

"I think I met her at the funeral. Dolores? My parents know who she is. Dad said he invited her to join us today?"

Zack nodded. "He did. Dolores had other plans. She always has other plans."

"Zack..."

He waved a hand to cut her off. "After my parents died, it was just Daphne and me. We swore we'd always be there for each other, no matter what. It was the two of us against the world. And when she met Robert, we widened the circle. And when Bobby and Karly were born, we widened it a little more. But it was always a pretty small circle."

"Oh Zack…"

His heart was pounding as if he'd been cliff jumping all morning instead of quietly baring his soul. Sharing the remembered pain was scarier than any of his wild adventures. Then Erin stepped closer and rested her head against his chest, wrapping both arms around his waist. He felt her hug all the way through his body, cradling him, soothing him, warming him right down to his toes.

Suddenly, he remembered his friend Mike standing on the deck of a South African boat and asking him what he wanted out of life. And now he knew. Finally.

This.

This is what I want.

This woman. This feeling of acceptance. Feeling like someone would be there to catch him when he fell. To help him with the kids. That he could help when she needed it too.

A feeling of belonging. Of *family.*

Somehow his arms were already wrapped around Erin, and he pulled her closer. "So, I've never asked anyone this before," he said, his voice rough. "But do you want to be my girlfriend?"

When she pulled her head away from his chest to look up at him, he could see tears glistening in her eyes. "Erin, why are you crying?

She sniffed and blinked her eyes, some of the moisture leaking out onto her cheeks. "You're not the guy I thought you were."

He stiffened. "No?"

She buried her head against his shirt again. "No," came the muffled reply. "You're even better."

He chuckled, something loosening in his chest. "Is that a yes? You'll be my girlfriend and dance with me at prom, all night long?"

"Or at least until midnight when they kick us out of the high school gym."

"All night long," he repeated, infusing his words with heated promise.

She sucked in a breath before nodding in agreement. "Okay."

One eyebrow pushed up. "Just okay?"

Her smile widened. "Well, we'll have to wait and see, won't we?"

CHAPTER 15

*E*very muscle in Erin's face ached. From smiling. And laughing. Her feet ached too, from all the dancing. Zack hadn't exaggerated his need to claim every dance, twirling her around on the gymnasium floor like it was his job.

When was the last time she'd had this much fun?

The attendees of the reunion "prom" were from several of the milestone graduating classes, from both Harwich and Chatham, so there was an interesting mix of those she didn't know and those she remembered from back in the day. A lot of familiar faces, since most of the attendees still lived locally, with Zack the most famous of the people who were there at the dance.

Seemed like everyone wanted to either shake his hand or get a selfie with the *Epic Adventures* guy. Erin thought Zack handled it well, smiling throughout, making tentative plans with some of his old lax buddies to grab lunch at the local sports pub one day soon.

At exactly midnight, the gym's overhead lights blazed to full strength and the music shut off. The high school slowly emptied, small scattered groups making plans for Sunday brunches and morning beach walks.

Erin followed Zack to his car, her hand firmly in his, her uncontrollable smile still in place as the full moon lit up the parking lot. "This was so much fun! I really didn't think I'd enjoy a fifteenth reunion this much."

He grinned at her, grey eyes sparkling in the bright moonlight. "What's not to enjoy? Especially since there was an actual bar at this prom, and not just punch spiked with cheap vodka."

She tipped her head from side to side, considering. "You know what I mean. Seeing people after all these years, some who you've seen around town, some you haven't seen since graduation. Everyone thinking they know you, since we all went to high school together. The catching up, the small talk, the justifications..."

Zack smirked. "Number one, I thought it was great to catch up with everyone."

She rolled her eyes and laughed. "Of course you would. You're living your dream. Television star who spends his time going on wild adventures in front of a camera. Everyone knows you."

He stopped next to the car, and pulled her closer. "Number two, they may think they know me. They know the character I play on TV. You're the only one who knows who I really am, that I'm struggling with this parenting stuff along with everyone else."

"Oh, poor baby. Is it tough that all they see is a sexy, fearless guy with six-pack abs and a lust for life?" She let her fingers trace a path down his chest, stopping at his belt buckle. "Was it weird to know every woman in there has seen you without your shirt on?"

Zack captured her fingers and brought them to his lips for a kiss. "Which brings me to number three for why tonight gets top marks. I got to spend the last six hours with you by my side, uninterrupted by small children demanding either of our attentions."

Her fingers tingled where his lips lingered. "Yeah, that part was pretty great."

"Great?" he scoffed. "I was hoping for better than great."

Erin grinned, feeling more than a little giddy, not sure if it was the wine going to her head or if it was all Zack. "The night is still young, Mr. Donovan. You have plenty of time to improve your score."

"Did you have anything specific in mind for me to earn extra credit?" He slipped one hand around to the back of her head and pulled her close for a kiss, warm and wicked and filled with the promise of more to come.

When he finally released her, she licked her lips and grinned again. "I can think of several things."

"Do I get a hint?" He opened the passenger door and helped her in. She could feel his gaze like a caress as he pointedly stared when those flirty pink ruffles on her dress slipped higher, exposing several inches of her bare thigh as she settled into the car seat.

She smiled up at him and licked her lips again, deciding she could be bold. She would ask for what she wanted. "You. Me. Naked. Bed."

His head flung back in laughter. "Now there's a word puzzle I can definitely figure out." He closed the passenger door and made his way to the driver's side. Starting up the car, he gave her a smoldering look. "I can't tell you how eager I am to get back to the house and see if I can talk you out of that dress."

"Spoiler alert," she said, even as a host of butterflies took flight in her gut. Honesty. She needed to lay all her cards on the table. "You're going to get lucky tonight. Although I have to warn you, it's been a while for me."

Pulling out of the parking lot, Zack kept to the speed limit. "It's been a while for me too."

She laid a hand on his leg and felt his thigh muscles tense. She decided to spell it out. "When I say it's been a while, I mean nearly seven years. I haven't had sex since Hailey was born."

His head jerked toward her, eyes wide. "Seriously?"

Erin shrugged, feeling self-conscious now. She looked out the window at the passing houses. "It's not a big deal. It's not like I was a hermit. I went out on dates a few times."

"But not…"

She shook her head. "After the whole thing with Leo, it was hard to trust anyone new. And then after Hailey got older and was more aware, I got a lot pickier about who I want to let into our lives. It's not just me to think about anymore." Since her hand was still on his leg, she squeezed his thigh. "I'll admit I'm nervous. I'm not sure I'll remember what to do. Sure, I understand the basics, the mechanics of sex, but the rest? I've got no game, as the high school kids say."

The car coasted to a stop at the red light in the middle of town. "Erin. Look at me."

She turned her head toward him, trying to keep her expression neutral.

"This is more than just a hook up. And we can take things as fast or as slow as you want."

She swallowed hard, feeling the butterflies in her stomach circle faster.

He quickly closed the space between them, leaning in to take her lips in a bruising kiss. One that left no room for arguments or second thoughts. This was happening.

THE PORCH LIGHTS BLAZED, illuminating the path across the yard. Erin waited for Zack to open the passenger door, taking her hand as they walked from the driveway to the front door. He'd left on the front hall lights as well, the house as warm and welcoming as always.

He closed the door behind her, before pushing her back up against it, caging her in with his arms and capturing her lips with his for a long, drugging kiss. When he pulled back, the heat in his eyes nearly melted her into a puddle before he leaned in and nibbled her earlobe.

"I want you, Erin Brannigan," his whispered, his breath hot against her ear. "I'll take however much you're willing to share with me."

"Take me to bed," she whispered back, letting her hands slide inside his suit jacket, pulling the dress shirt loose from his pants so she could touch bare skin. *Hot, smooth, perfect.*

He groaned as she let her fingernails trail lightly up his back. "Keep doing that and we aren't going to make it to the bedroom."

Grabbing his hand, she dragged him toward the staircase, laughing. "We're not having sex for the first time on the couch where the kids hang out and watch cartoons."

"Nope. Not gonna go there." He ignored her squeals of protest, scooping her up and carrying her up to the second floor, depositing her on the bed and taking a step back to fully divest himself of the suit jacket.

She propped herself up on her elbows to watch the show, kicking off her heels, letting them fall to the floor. The familiar pale blue walls and ceiling fan reminded her of the morning not that long ago when she'd woken in this bed, fully dressed and alone, not at all sure how she'd gotten there. Tonight, she'd studiously avoided the tequila and planned to remember every minute.

Every. Single. Moment.

"Still too many clothes," she told him as he threw the jacket over the back of the chair in the corner with a flourish.

He smirked. "I could say the same about you."

"Oh yeah? What are you gonna do about it?"

He stalked over to the bed, slipping off his tie and undoing the buttons on his shirt one by one with each slow step. Her mouth went dry as she finally – finally – got to see that magnificent chest of his up close and in person.

"Oh God, look at you," she thought and said at the same time. "Better than on TV."

"Look later," he said, his voice almost a growl. He pulled her up to her feet and turned her, sliding the zipper down the back of her pink dress. "I've been dying to pull on this zipper all night long." He pushed the fabric off her shoulders, letting it pool around her hips, sliding his hands up the bare skin of her back and around to cup her lace-covered breasts.

"Beautiful," he whispered. He spun her again, bending to plant open mouth kisses on one breast and then the other right through the lace. When he used his teeth to gently nip, she gasped, feeling the tug of it all the way to her core.

She slid her hands along the hard muscles of his back as he lavished attention on her nipples, releasing the catch on her bra and pushing it out of the way so that his tongue and teeth connected with bare skin. Heat and lust filled her in a way she'd never felt before, her entire body vibrating with energy and need. Everything felt so new and yet so familiar. So right. As if she'd been waiting all her life to have his hands on her body, and hers on his.

When he finally pushed the dress the rest of the way to the floor, she stepped out of it and for a moment felt self-consciousness, suddenly aware she was naked except for tiny lace undies, sure that her body was too soft around the middle. Not model thin like the women pictured in the tabloids with Zack. She wrapped her arms around her hips and stomach, but he pulled them away.

"Don't do that," he said. "Don't hide from me."

She felt her cheeks heat. "Having a baby changes… things," she said, looking away.

His fingers gripped her chin, forcing her to meet his eyes. "Not for me. You're perfect just the way you are." He dipped his head and took her mouth in another long, heated kiss, tongues tangling, stroking, reassuring her that she was beautiful and wanted, oh so wanted.

She fumbled with his belt, letting it finally fall to the floor with a thud, the pants disappearing an instant later, boxer briefs quick to follow. His cock jutted out and up, long and proud, and she wrapped eager fingers around his thickness, eliciting a sharp gasp from Zack.

"Not yet," he said, capturing her hand in his larger one. "Or this will be over before we even get started." He gently urged her back onto the bed, holding both of her hands over her head. He lavished more attention on her breasts until she squirmed underneath him, needing more.

As if reading her mind, he kissed his way down her torso, spreading her thighs wide.

"You don't have to…" she started.

He cut her off. "Oh, but I want to. I desperately want to taste you." He ducked his head, pushing the thin barrier to one side as his tongue slowly licked her center, sending her eyes rolling back into her head.

"Unless you don't like this…" his voice trailed off as she pulled her hands free and tunneled her fingers into his hair.

"Don't you dare stop now," she whispered, tugging at his hair.

He lifted his head despite the pressure from her hands. "I don't intend to stop." He nipped her thigh, soothing the hurt with his tongue, before tracing a path back to her center. "But I'm going to owe you a new thong," he said, as he tugged on the lace and it ripped away. Licking, sucking, teasing... she rode the wave, higher and higher, until he pushed one thick finger into her slick core, crooking it to touch that magic spot deep inside, sending her spiraling up into the universe.

Slowly, she came back to earth, hearing the crinkle of a condom wrapper, then the feel of all that hard body pressed against her. When he drove into her, the world didn't simply move. It was like a tornado blowing through, again sending all of her senses spiraling, swirling her emotions into a perfect storm, up, up, up, until she shattered into a million pieces of light, raining slowly back down into the room.

This. This is what she'd been missing all her life. Not even when things with Leo were good had she ever felt this bliss. This sense of perfect connection... the kind she felt now with Zack.

He rolled to his side, pulling her body tight to his. "That was..."

"Incredible. Perfect. More than perfect." She hadn't fully caught her breath when she pressed a kiss against his throat. "You are more than perfect."

He chuckled, also sounding out of breath. "That's not what you would have said a month ago."

She shifted to face him. "What do you mean?"

"All our arguments over me trying to parent Bobby and Karly." He looked up at the ceiling. "You were right, though. What did I know about being a parent? Almost nothing. I'm learning as I go. I'd like to think I'm doing my best with a bad situation."

"Oh Zack." Her heart squeezed painfully, hearing the underlying doubt in his voice. "None of us have a playbook to this parenting thing. We're all just doing the best that we can, and reaching out for help when we need it."

He pulled her tighter to him. "I'm doing better with your help. I'm better with you by my side."

"I like being at your side." She shifted to kiss his lips, just a gentle touch, to let him know she was with him.

"I like being at your side, too." He kissed her back, taking the kiss deeper. Rolling her onto her back, tongues tangling. His voice was a rough whisper as he added, "I like being inside you, too."

Which he proceeded to show her. Again.

And again.

CHAPTER 16

December

Parked cars lined both sides of the street as Zack drove slowly toward the Brannigan house, Bobby and Karly offering running commentary from the minivan's second row seats.

"Are all these cars for Hailey's birthday party? Are we late? Why are we always late for everything?" Karly kicked the back of Zack's seat when he didn't answer fast enough. "Uncle Z? Why is the driver still sitting in that long black car thing? Is he late too?"

Bobby answered for him. "That's called a *lim-oh-zeen*, not a car thing. And regular people don't drive them, they rent them and pay for a professional driver."

Karly kicked the back of Zack's seat again. "Uncle Z is our professional driver."

Zack huffed out a laugh as the minivan passed the long black limo. He spotted an opening further up the road and finally parked the car. "The Brannigans are having a holiday open house along with Hailey's birthday party, so there will be lots of people at the house. You two need to promise me you'll be on your best behavior."

"We promise, Uncle Z," came the chorus from the backseat. He heard them fussing with their restraints, Bobby helping Karly to unsnap the arm straps of her car seat.

"Bobby, don't forget the present," he reminded the boy before he got out of the car. He circled around to the back and opened the rear hatch. He'd been tasked with picking up the cake from the specialty bakery in Hyannis, an elaborate confection shaped like a pirate ship that Hailey was going to absolutely go crazy for. Unfortunately, the holiday traffic made them a little late to the party. He'd meant to arrive before Leo.

In the three weeks since Thanksgiving, Zack had spent a lot of time with Erin and knew she was nervous about Hailey's father finally coming to Cape Cod. About her daughter's reaction to meeting him. About seeing the guy again after seven years.

And after three weeks of laughing with her and making love with her, Zack couldn't fathom how anyone in their right mind could have walked away from her. Ever. But especially not when she was pregnant.

What kind of guy does that?

He'd had his fair share of sex over the years, but it was always just sex. He'd never enjoyed hanging out with any of those women, or talking with them. He'd never laughed with anyone as much as he had with Erin over the last few weeks. At Thanksgiving with her family, and at prom with old friends. At the Christmas stroll with all three kids in tow, running into all the other teachers and friends from school. Even while waiting in line to let the kids sit on Santa's lap, they'd kept each other amused telling silly knock-knock jokes, Zack laughing more than all three kids combined.

And in bed late at night, after everyone was fast asleep and it was just the two of them, pleasuring each other. The sex was good. Being totally honest he had to admit the sex was amazing and the best he'd ever had. On top of that, above and beyond that, he felt closer to Erin than he'd ever felt to another person. Chemistry, connection, whatever you want to call it. Even when he first came home and every interaction had been a fight, the spark had been there, arcing between them.

How had his life changed so completely in only a few short weeks?

And he wanted more. More laughter, more kisses, more quiet moments shared together.

More of everything.

And Leo Kensington had willingly walked away from all of it.

Asshole.

"Hurry up already, Uncle Z," Bobby called from up ahead on the sidewalk. He held the gift bag in one hand, and Karly's hand in his other.

"You don't want me to drop the cake, do you?"

"Okay fine." Bobby exhaled an overly dramatic sigh. "But this means we get to stay longer at the end."

"Sounds good to me, kiddo." Zack already planned to stay at least until after Leo Kensington left the party, and then make sure that Erin felt okay about the whole encounter. After all the help and support she'd given him over the last month, it felt like the least he could do for the woman he loved.

He stumbled on the front walk, almost dropping the cake. *Love?*

Holy shit! Love! He loved her. The thought warmed him all over and scared him silly at the same time. Because, wow. *Love.* But now that he'd realized it, called it by the right name, he couldn't figure out how it took him so long to get to this place. Of course he loved her. *And how scary is that?*

When she'd said those words to him a few nights ago, spooning in bed after a round of truly mind-blowing sex, he hadn't responded. He assumed the post-sex endorphins caused the words to tumble from those luscious lips of hers. It was too soon for love to be part of the equation between them. So he didn't respond. And she didn't repeat them. But... what if she meant it? What if she had already reached this place of understanding the connection between them was the real deal?

Love. Forever. What a concept.

He pushed the thoughts aside, good and bad, figuring they had no place in today's pirate festivities for a seven-year-old's birthday. Erin was anxious enough about today. He could wait to lay those feelings on her until after the party ended. Maybe tonight in bed. Maybe tomorrow over coffee and kisses. He could wait to share his revelation, but not too long.

Because yeah, he loved her.

Erin herself greeted them at the door, her blond hair pulled back in a bouncy ponytail, her jeans and red V-neck sweater hugging all those tantalizing curves he'd recently come to know so intimately. But the smile on her beautiful face spread too wide, too fake, the tension already visible in her eyes, in her voice.

The thought that she was stressed made his heart clench, made him want to fix things.

Because I love her. The thought got less scary each time it ran through his mind.

"Hey Bobby and Karly! The kids are all in the backyard getting ready to bash the pinata, just waiting for you two to get here. Go right on out through the kitchen."

"Wait a sec." Zack shot Bobby a warning look before asking, "Are there adults out there with the pinata, in charge of said bashing?"

Erin's smile looked overly bright. "Why, yes there are, Mr. Safety First. Stephanie and her husband are in charge, and a few other parents are out there too. The kids are in good hands, trust me."

Zack nodded to Bobby and Karly, who wasted no time getting outside to join the fun.

After the kids ran down the hall, Erin let the fake smile drop, replaced with one of relief and gratitude. "Thank you so much for picking up the cake, Zack. I had a plan, really I did, but then Leo showed up early, and my mom kind of flaked out, and... things spiraled out of my control. I know traffic to and from Hyannis was probably awful today, because of the town's holiday 'buy local' stroll."

He followed her to the dining room, bypassing the noisy living room where Maureen and Tom's friends and neighbors crowded, drinking spiked cider and sharing holiday cheer. He merely nodded at

Tom in passing, unwilling to take either of his hands off the cake. Maureen came out into the hallway, giving him a quick kiss on the cheek before turning to her daughter.

"Have they started the pinata yet? I wanted to get some pictures. Maybe a video."

"They're all outside, Mom. And video would be awesome. I can't believe I didn't think of that."

"I'm on it." With a last quick wink at Zack, Maureen went outside, her red skirts swishing in her wake.

Erin sighed, watching her go. "We've always held the birthday and the holiday open house on the same day every December. It made sense before, but this year…"

If his hands weren't already carrying the cake, he'd be wrapping them around her. "Seems like everyone is having fun. I'm sorry we took so long getting here. We should've been here to help you." He placed the cake box in the middle of the long dining room table.

She removed the lid and folded down the sides of the box. A genuine smile lit her features as she admired the pirate ship, with its tall masts and billowing sails. "Oh, they did such a nice job! This turned out really great. How do you think they get the cloth to stay puffed out like they're filled with wind?"

"Ah, the cake delivery is finally here." A cultured British accent preceded the man entering the room. He wore leather riding boots, wool pants and a tweed jacket, complete with elbow patches. "What do we owe you for making such a fine cake for our daughter?

Our daughter.

The infamous Leo. Zack narrowed his eyes, scanning him top to toe, taking an instant dislike to everything about him. Tall, but not as tall as Zack, he noted with some satisfaction. Gym fit, with the wiry build of a cyclist. Shortish, light brown hair in that purposefully messy style that took hours and tons of product to achieve. Eyes the pale blue of ice chips, and just as warm. Dressed for a hunt in the English country-side, not a Cape Cod birthday party full of kindergarteners and their parents.

The prick pulled a fat leather wallet from his pocket as he stepped closer. "Come, come, good man. Don't be shy. Name your price. Everyone has to make a living."

Erin intervened, placing a hand flat on Leo's chest to stop the advance. "Leo, stop. I told you my friend was picking up the cake for me."

Friend? Is that how she explained their relationship? The sudden urge to stake his claim to this woman, the woman he loved, burned through him. He reached an arm around her waist and pulled her back against his chest, placing a soft kiss just above her ear.

He saw Leo's eyes track the move and narrow to slits. Then the asshole smiled, showing all his perfect teeth. "Right. The chap who likes adventures." He stuck out his right hand. "Leo Kensington, pleasure to meet you."

Forced into a polite response, Zack released his hold on Erin and shook the man's hand. Soft, manicured, cultured like his accent. "Zack Donovan. I've heard a lot about you, Leo."

"Sorry I can't say the same about you, mate."

Erin turned toward Zack now, placing that flat palm on his chest, where it belonged. Her low voice held a note of pleading. "Play nice, for Hailey's sake. Remember what we talked about."

Right. Erin wanted to give Hailey the opportunity to meet her father, and form her own impressions of the man. Ask her own questions, get her own answers.

He looked into her upturned eyes, and gave a quick nod. He didn't plan to cause any trouble or make a scene. He cleared his throat. "I think I'll go out back and say hello to the other parents, check how the pirates are getting along."

Erin visibly relaxed. "After the pinata, the treasure hunt will begin. Your pirate gear is waiting for you in the kitchen. Hailey's been telling absolutely everyone that the famous Zack Donovan will lead them on an *epic adventure.*"

"Yes indeed. So handy to have a famous explorer on tap who's willing to do children's parties," Leo drawled. "Whatever you're charging it should be worth the cost."

Zack ignored him, focusing on Erin. "I've got this."

"I know you do."

He pressed a gentle kiss to her forehead, both to reassure her that he had her back, and to annoy Leo. When he left the room, he noted the other man clenching both hands into fists.

Good. Zack didn't plan to cause trouble, but he wasn't going to cut the guy any slack. Not a single inch. This was the man who kicked Erin to the curb when she found out she was pregnant. Now he'd decided he wanted her and Hailey back?

Too fucking late, mate. She's mine now.

CHAPTER 17

*E*rin watched Zack leave the room. Part of her wished she could stay plastered by his side for the whole party and not have to deal with her ex's bullshit, but that was cowardly thinking. She owed it to Hailey to be civil to the girl's father. Erin might have her own opinions of Leo as a dad, but her daughter needed the chance to form opinions of her own.

The man had traveled all this way to finally meet his daughter. Being polite was the least she could do in return. If the last two hours in his presence were any indication, staying civil shouldn't be all that difficult. Or at least, no more difficult than dealing with some of the parents at school. Or having a root canal.

Not fun, but something that could be endured. Something that had to be done.

"So that's the wanker you've replaced me with, is it?"

Leo's question drew her attention back to him. He'd shoved both hands into his pockets and rocked back on the heels of his ridiculous looking riding boots. The Leo she remembered wore jeans and t-shirts. Expensive designer jeans, of course, but not outfits like this one that belonged in a magazine spread from *Town & Country*.

"That's the man I'm dating, yes." She squared her shoulders and looked him in the eye. "And I didn't replace you, Leo. You shoved me out the door."

He rolled his eyes. "Yes, yes. But I apologized for that, love. You said on the phone you forgave me."

"I did. I do." She blew out a breath and shook her head. "Listen, I don't want to fight with you. Let's go outside and enjoy the party, shall we?"

"Whatever you desire," he agreed with a smile, taking her hand.

She knew she should have pulled her hand back sooner, when she saw Zack eyeballing them as soon as they stepped onto the deck. He was across the lawn, chatting with a few of the other fathers. His disapproving frown made her pull her hand away from Leo's, using it to gesture at the kids taking turns bashing at a pinata shaped like a treasure chest.

"Do they do this sort of thing at birthday parties in England? Pinatas, I mean."

"Not at the sort of parties I've been to," Leo admitted, stepping forward to place both hands on the railing surrounding the deck. "Then again, this is my first children's birthday party."

"Right. No nieces or nephews?"

He shook his head, focused on the child swinging the bat. "Only child, remember? I believe my cousin Reginald has a boy, but he's since moved to Wales. I'm certainly not trekking across the country for soggy cake and balloons."

"You flew across an ocean for a piece of this birthday cake," she pointed out.

"Ah, but this is different. This is my daughter." He turned to face her again. "I've missed so much already. Years of parties like this that I can't get back."

"True." Erin sighed and let herself relax a little. "Although, to be honest, this is her first big birthday party because she's in school now, so you haven't missed too much in way of big celebrations."

"Good to know," he said with a nod. "Hard to believe she's old enough to go off to school. Feels like just yesterday when you and I were banging around Soho and Hackney Wick." He rattled off the names of their old London stomping grounds with a smile that said the memories were good.

Erin remembered the good times, but she also remembered the bad. The times he stayed out all night, only to stumble back to the flat the following morning reeking of alcohol and another woman's perfume. Returning to London after a trip to see her family, only to find favorite clothing missing from her closet, or unfamiliar underwear in their shared laundry hamper. He was an artist, with an artistic temperament and a talent for bullshit. Every time he convinced her that she was imaging things. Or that the other women were just friends of his, other artists. That none of them meant anything to him.

She'd let so many things slide, because in the end it wasn't as if they were married.

Until the day she found out her birth control had failed, and choices had to be made.

She made one choice. Leo made another.

"Come on," she said, starting down the stairs. She was happy with the choices she'd made, and had no desire to change any of them. "Let's join the party."

THE PINATA BASHING went off without anyone getting hurt, either with the bashing itself or in the chaotic scramble to grab candy once the thing finally cracked apart spilling mini candy bars across the lawn. Zack was absolutely brilliant as the head pirate, complete with eye patch and shiver-me-timbers pirate jargon, leading the band of swashbuckling kindergarteners to work together, following clues to find their prizes. Most of the adults came out of the house and gathered on the deck to watch the fun. Several commented to her on how great Zack was with the kids, some of the women also whispering questions about her English prince. Apparently, he'd been introducing himself as *Lord Kensington*.

"He's not *my prince*, or even an actual prince," she whispered back to those few. "He's just a guy I used to date."

"And Hailey's father," her friends all reminded her.

"And Hailey's father," her mother reminded her.

As if she could forget.

Finally – *finally* – the organized games were finished, the song was sung, the cake was cut and served, and the kids all disappeared to play in the basement playroom, where the Brannigans had a bumper pool table, an old-fashioned pinball machine, and more toys than any home should, collected over the years to entertain all the cousins during family gatherings.

Adults still milled about the upstairs rooms, enjoying the beer, wine, and spiked cider her parents served. Erin shoved the last of the pirate-themed cake plates in the garbage bag, eager to find Zack and have a glass of wine before other parents started to leave. He'd told her he would stay until the party was finished. She couldn't wait to put her feet up and snuggle next to him on the couch while their kids – hers and his – watched their favorite pirate movie yet again. The perfect end to a pirate party.

As she washed the last bits of stubborn frosting from her hands, Leo entered the kitchen with two glasses of white wine. "I thought you might need one of these after all the work you put into this kiddie bash."

She dried her hands on a dishtowel before accepting the offered glass. "Thanks, that's very thoughtful of you. I'm sorry you haven't had much time alone with Hailey today. Everything's been so hectic."

Leaning back against the counter, Leo chuckled. "No worries at all. Quite surprising to see all the little nippers running about the place, like a pack of wild animals with megaphones instead of normal voices. That daughter of ours is a whirlwind of activity. Is she always this... enthusiastic?"

Erin leaned against the counter opposite to Leo and took a large swallow of the crisp Sauvignon Blanc. "I think all the excitement and sugar had something to do with the noise levels today, but honestly? Yes. Hailey's always quite energetic, running since she first learned to walk."

Leo twirled the stem of his wine glass, the golden liquid sparkling as it moved. "Erin. I know I bumbled things up when you first told me about the baby. I figured we had a good thing going and why make any changes? I liked our life the way it was. I realize now, you were right to leave me. Right to keep the baby."

She pressed her lips together, not sure what to say in response. Instead, she took another big gulp of wine.

He placed his wine glass on the countertop, sliding his hands into his jacket pockets and taking a step closer to where she stood. "I know you turned me down when I asked over the phone, but now that I'm here, now that I've met my daughter in person, I'm going to ask again. Would you ever consider coming back to England?"

"Leo, I told you before. I like my life the way it is now. I don't see how I can uproot Hailey from everything and everyone she knows."

The look on his face was determined. "I understand. It's a risk to make a big move like that without some kind of incentive." He took a step closer, before lowering one knee down to the kitchen floor.

Erin stared at him, confused. "Leo, what are you doing?"

"I'm bending the knee, as they say." He pulled his hands from his pockets, a small velvet box in one. He opened it to reveal a sparkling diamond the size of a quarter, nestled in a setting covered with a double row of smaller diamonds all around the band. He held it out for her inspection, the reflected shine almost blinding.

"Leo…"

"Marry me, Erin Brannigan, and make me the luckiest man in Surrey. In all of England. All of the world. Let us be a family. You, me, and Hailey. A real family."

"Oh Leo…"

"Hear me out first, love. This was my grandmother's ring, the Duchess of Surrey. Do you remember meeting her?"

She vaguely remembered the older woman with the perpetual sour look on her face. If Leo's parents had been cold to Erin, the grandmother had been arctic. She opened her mouth to say so but he waved off her words.

"Never mind that for now. The fact is, she gave the ring to me before she died, and told me to find you and bring you back to England. You and my daughter. And here I am, ready to do whatever it takes for you to come home with me. To fulfill the last wishes of my dying grandmother. Erin, come home." He stayed on bent knee, looking up at her expectantly.

For one long protracted moment, she was at a total loss for words. She said the first thing that came to mind. "Your grandmother hated me."

Leo smiled, his eyes crinkling in the corners. "Not true, love. She didn't hate you, particularly. She disliked people in general."

"But you said she gave you that ring, told you to propose to me?"

His head tipped from side to side. "Something like that, yeah. So what do you say? Will you marry me?"

"No, Leo, I'm not going to marry you." Erin took the last gulp of her wine and put her glass on the counter next to the sink.

"Why not?"

"I don't love you. And you don't love me." She crossed her arms over her chest. "And please stand up before someone sees you like this."

He pushed up to standing, letting the ring box close with a loud snap. "Love has nothing to do with marriage. We like each other, we have a child together, isn't that enough?"

"Not for me." Erin shook her head to emphasize her point, wishing she had another glass of wine handy for this conversation. "Why now, Leo? You've ignored us for seven years. What changed?"

He picked up his wineglass and chugged the rest of the liquid. "Grandmother died."

"And?"

"And her will says I can't get my inheritance until I settle down, marry, and produce an heir. I thought if you were willing to marry me, I could throw a massive Christmas bash at the family estate to celebrate our wedding, and get my inheritance before New Years."

Stunned by his honesty, all Erin could do was stare. "But... But I thought you were planning to stay on Cape Cod through the holidays?"

He had the decency to look embarrassed. "I may have said something to that effect. But I really thought once you saw the ring, saw that I was indeed serious, you'd forget about our past indiscretions and say yes to marriage. There's a limo waiting outside to whisk the three of us back to Boston airport."

"Are you for real? Leo, you don't want to marry me. You cheated on me the entire time we were together in London. Marry one of those women."

"None of them had the forethought to get up the duff. I need an heir to fulfill the requirements of Grandmother's inheritance. Coming here, to you, seemed the most expedient way." He opened the fridge and grabbed another open bottle of white wine, sloshing a healthy portion into his glass before offering the bottle to her. "Grandmother may not have approved of you, but she knew about the baby. She made sure to have the family solicitor send a check every year on the girl's birthday. Hailey is a Kensington, after all."

She took the bottle from him, wondering whether it was a good idea to have another drink with this man, or whether she should kick him to the curb – *and his waiting limo* – immediately. She'd previously thought the annual card and check didn't arrive because Leo himself was coming in person. It never occurred to her that the grandmother orchestrated the gifting. And now the woman was dead.

Her next thought was *poor Hailey!* The child spent all last week so excited to meet her father, and would be heartbroken when she found out he only considered her *expedient* in claiming his fortune.

"You should say good-bye to your daughter before you leave," Erin said, her voice calm. She poured more wine into her glass and placed the empty bottle on the counter. "Now that she's met you, she'll want to keep in touch. I have your email address so she can write to you."

"So that's it then? You won't even consider my marriage proposal?" Leo drained the rest of his wine in one long gulp.

"I did consider it. I said no," Erin said calmly. "And now I'm telling you that you should leave, so you don't miss your flight."

"I don't understand why you wouldn't want a Christmas wedding."

A squeak of shocked surprise turned both their attention to the doorway. Hailey stood like a statue, holding open the kitchen door. "Who's getting married?"

"No one, sweetie." Erin strode across the room to her daughter. "Why aren't you playing with your friends in the playroom?"

"Bobby just left. He said Karly had to go home to bed. I thought you said they were staying later and we could watch movies after everyone else left? And why are you two in the kitchen alone talking about weddings?"

Leo placed his empty glass on the counter, smirking at Erin before telling Hailey, "I asked your mother to marry me so we can be a real family. Wouldn't you like that, sweetheart?"

Hailey's nose crinkled. "Why would Mom *marry* you? She doesn't love *you*, she loves Zack."

"Because I'm your father, of course," Leo said, as if it were the most obvious thing in the world.

"So what?" Hailey fisted her hands on her hips and glared at the man. "You don't love her, or me. Zack does."

Erin felt her heart swell with love for this strong, independent child she'd raised, and put an arm around the girl's shoulders to face Leo in solidarity. "I think you have your answer now, Leo. Your limo is waiting."

Hailey's tough stance wavered. "Wait, you're leaving already? I thought you were staying all week? Staying until Christmas?"

His laugh sounded mean. "Why stay if you don't want what I'm offering? We could be a family. Live in a castle in the English countryside. But you're choosing the action hero instead of your actual father. Good luck with that." His shoulders brushed against Erin's as he passed, heading out of the kitchen and down the hallway.

Hailey looked up at her mother, her lower lip trembling. "He's really leaving? What did I do wrong?"

Erin sighed, deciding to be honest. The child deserved honesty from at least one parent. "He never intended to stay for Christmas. He was always going to fly back to England tonight."

"But he wanted us to go with him? To be a family, like he said?"

"It's complicated," Erin told her.

"Is that why Zack left with Bobby and Karly? Because of my father?"

Erin wasn't sure. Could Zack have overheard Leo's proposal? Even if he did, Zack knew her history with the man. Knew she didn't love him and wouldn't ever say yes. Didn't he?

"I don't know why he left, honey. Maybe Karly was really tired and he didn't want to risk a tantrum ruining the rest of your party."

Hailey nodded slowly. "Okay. And after everyone leaves, you'll call him and make it all better."

"Absolutely."

She hugged her daughter to her side, hoping it was as simple as that.

CHAPTER 18

*E*veryone leaves.

Zack took another gulp of whiskey, focusing on the burn as it traveled down his throat and splashed into his mostly empty stomach.

He'd locked down his emotions and held it together for the sake of the kids. The party had been mostly over when he told Bobby they needed to get Karly home to bed instead of staying longer. The boy ran off to hug the birthday girl good-bye and they were able to leave without much fanfare.

He couldn't bring himself to talk to Erin. Not now.

Not after overhearing what he did.

Not after seeing that monster of a diamond the asshole proposed with. How could he ever compete with that?

She was going back to England to marry that aristocratic twat. Off to play lord and lady of the manor with her baby daddy. Leaving Cape Cod for good.

Leaving him.

With the kids now safely tucked away in bed, he and this bottle were going to spend the rest of the night getting acquainted, burning away all the raw emotions threatening to overwhelm him. Feelings he hadn't allowed himself to indulge until recently. Until her.

For good reason, as it turns out.

Because everyone leaves.

Even though she told him she loved him, she was still going to leave.

When his cell phone rang, he thought about not answering it. Probably Erin again, wondering why he'd left. He let the last two calls go to voicemail, which he didn't bother listening to. Did he want to confront her? Or just keep ignoring her calls until she scampered off to jolly old England with her prince?

He checked the screen, ready to confront her, but it wasn't her. It was Mike.

He'd had enough whiskey to think it a good idea to talk with his buddy. Maybe invite him to visit Cape Cod for Christmas.

"Mike, my old buddy, old pal, as Jimmy Stewart would say! What's going on?"

There was a pause. "Zack, are you drunk?"

"Not yet, but I'm hoping to be soon," he answered and took another gulp of the whiskey.

"Is everything okay?"

"I dunno. You tell me. Oh hey, before I forget, do you wanna come spend Christmas with me and the kids here on the Cape? Go watch the light parade of boats on the harbor? Dress up like Santa and surf the waves at Nauset Beach? Wouldn't that be great for a Christmas episode?"

"Is that what you and Erin plan to do for the holidays?"

"Pffffftt. That's over." Zack took another swig of whiskey, barely feeling the burn this time. "There's no *me and Erin* any more. I've got more important things to focus on, like our show. Speaking of which, what did the network suit say about the new idea I emailed everyone about? Did you pitch it in person?"

"You mean your idea about focusing the show on more family-friendly adventures?"

"Yeah, that's the one. I'm telling you, Mike. I think it's an untapped goldmine of possibilities. Family vacations these days are about more than going to theme parks or sitting on a beach somewhere. We'd be tapping a whole new demographic, and a whole new avenue for advertising dollars."

Mike grunted. "The executives were a bit peeved you didn't make it to New York to pitch the idea in person."

"I told you, not while school is in session. I explained…"

"And they understood. To a point. They gave us a tentative green light for the project. But."

"But what?"

"They want a proof of concept."

"What the fuck does that mean? What kind of proof?"

"Like one full episode, right away. To see how it plays out."

His anger from earlier surged back through Zack. "*How it plays out*? Again, what the fuck does that mean?"

"Zack. You're not what the network would call a *family man*. They've never seen you interact with kids. How do they know your single-guy sex appeal with the 25-65 demographic will translate to the new concept? Or how you'll look on camera with kids in tow? How that'll change the image, both yours and the show?"

"Of course the show is going to change. It's got to. It'll still be *Epic Adventures*, but different. Like, *Epic Adventures, Family Edition*."

Another pause, this one shorter. He heard the smile in Mike's voice when he finally said, "Actually, I like that for a show title. I like that a lot."

"Yeah?" The anger dissipated and Zack felt hope stirring in its place.

Mike continued. "Yeah. And I can picture you rocking that single dad vibe. Hey, maybe we can invite different single moms with their kids to join each adventure, and it'll be like *The Bachelor* on steroids."

Zack grimaced at the thought. "No. No more single moms."

"But you said you and Erin were finished, right?"

"Doesn't mean I'm jumping back into the dating pool. Not anytime soon, at least." *Or ever.* Just because Erin could turn off her feelings so quickly and move on to marry someone else didn't mean he could. Or should. Or would.

"Fine." Mike sighed, and let silence fill the space between them for another long minute. "Hey, how about this. Instead of me coming to Cape Cod for Christmas, let's get the crew together and go somewhere warm, film that last spring episode and make it the proof of concept for the new season. Two birds with one stone kind of thing."

"Brilliant! That's a great idea!" Zack jumped up to grab his laptop from the kitchen counter. Signing in quickly, he pulled up a browser and typed in *family friendly island vacations*. "Somewhere in Mexico or the Caribbean? What do you think?"

"The resorts in Mexico all make a big deal about Christmas, so not a good choice for a late spring episode," Mike said. Zack could hear him clacking away on his own laptop.

Zack scanned his search results, a sense of excitement replacing some of the darkness as he started to picture the way it might play out. "What about Turks and Caicos? Third largest coral reef in the world, lots of family friendly resorts, tons of shit to do with kids… pull it up and take a look."

The sounds of Mike typing filled the silence. "Yeah, this could work. Yeah, I think we're onto something with this."

"If the network green lights the initial episode, we can spend the summer school vacation filming the fall season. Maybe each season could have a theme, like a section of the U.S. You know, like a season focused on New England adventures."

"Or a season of visiting National Parks."

"Or a season of driving cross country, coast to coast. Route 66, family style."

"Dude, we can come up with a ton of season themes if they buy into this first episode!" Mike's voice conveyed the same excitement he felt, and Zack couldn't help but grin.

This was going to work.

He could be the guardian Bobby and Karly needed, and still keep his show alive and well. Maybe even make it better. The kids would absolutely love traveling with him, going on adventures together. Except...

"Shit. My sister's in-laws are supposed to come to visit us for the holidays. Spend time with the kids." What would Agnes think of his plan to drag her grandchildren all over the world on adventures?

"Invite them to come to Turks and Caicos with us. If they want, we could even include them in the filming. Don't some families bring the grandparents along when they travel?"

Zack laughed out loud at the thought of Agnes snorkeling the coral reef with the kids. "I'm afraid they aren't that sort of grand-parents."

"Invite them anyway."

"Yeah, I think I will."

Before hanging up, Zack and Mike made plans to touch base again the following day, after Mike ran the idea and some budgetary numbers past the showrunner and the network suits. Zack hung up the phone feeling better than he had all day.

He had a solid plan. Now he just needed to get Agnes on board. He didn't want to fight a custody battle against her, not when he knew in his heart he could offer his niece and nephew a better life than they'd have in Florida with their grandparents.

He took a deep breath, and dialed Agnes's number.

An hour later, after a long and at times difficult conversation, Zack hung up the phone. Agnes and Richard might not be fully convinced, but they were willing to go along with a Christmas trip to the islands rather than Cape Cod. Agnes was anxious to see how the grandkids were holding up, but seemed willing to go along with Zack's new plan and the new direction for his show. One that was more family oriented, and didn't include teaching Bobby how to wrestle alligators.

He searched online for flights and last-minute resort bookings while they talked, and finally got her off the phone, promising that they would see her at the Florida airport soon enough, and from there travel together. Whether or not the network gave a green light to next season, they were going to film one more episode for next spring. And it would happen in Turks and Caicos.

Clicking send on one last email to Mike, Zack shut down his laptop and went upstairs to check on the kids. If they were still awake, he could tell them about this new plan for the holidays, let them get excited about something before he shared the other news.

It was going to be hard, especially for Bobby, when Hailey and her mom left for England. Not only had Bobby bonded with the little girl, but he loved his teacher. A Christmas getaway would help ease both the loss of a friend and the classroom transition for the boy.

And just like that, his mood began to spiral back into darkness.

Zack wasn't sure if the trip would ease anything for him, or make it any easier to let Erin go. But it's not like she'd given him any choice in the matter. She was leaving. He'd just have to get used to the idea. No matter how much it hurt.

The light was on in Bobby's room, but when he stepped through the doorway it was empty. Not in bed, not at his desk, not playing with his toys in the corner by the closet. Empty. A quick glance down the hallway showed the bathroom door open, the lights in there off.

He ran to Karly's room and flipped on the overhead light. "Karly. Is Bobby in here with you?"

"No." She sat up in bed, rubbing her eyes. "He said he doesn't want to go to Florida."

Zack felt his heart rate double. "What do you mean? No one is going to Florida. Where is he hiding?"

"He left." She crossed her arms over her chest and stared back at him from her bed.

"Left?" Zack's heart sank to the pit of his stomach. "Left his room?"

"He said he was leaving for good. That I should go with him, but I'm too tired right now to walk anywhere."

"Karly. Tell me exactly what he said."

"He said he heard you talking to Grandma and you're taking us to Florida. He said he doesn't want to go. That he wanted to live with a family who wouldn't leave him behind."

His heart squeezed tight. He understood that feeling all too well.

"Karly. You know that you and Bobby are the most important things to me, don't you?"

The skeptical look on her little face told him she wasn't convinced of that fact. "What about your show?"

"I'm trying to figure out a way for us all to go on adventures together."

"Like a family?"

"That's exactly what I mean. You, me, and Bobby. You're my family. I'm not leaving you guys behind."

She jumped out of bed and crossed the room in two seconds, leaping up into his waiting arms and burying her head against his chest.

He hugged her tight. "I love you, Karly. You belong to me now."

"You mean we belong to each other," she whispered back.

"Yeah, that's exactly what I mean."

Zack's cell phone dinged, signaling a new text. Without putting Karly down, he pulled it from his front pocket. Erin. *I think I found something you lost.*

"C'mon, Karly. Let's go get your brother back."

CHAPTER 19

$\mathcal{T}$he sharp knock on the front door let her know he'd arrived. With a last glance toward the kitchen, where Hailey and Bobby sat having hot chocolate with her mom, Erin opened the door.

In the circle of brightness cast by the porch lights, Zack and Karly stood holding hands.

Not meeting Zack's eyes, Erin crouched down to Karly's level. "Hey sweetie, Bobby and Hailey are in the kitchen having cocoa if you want to join them."

"That's not what we're here to…"

Before Zack could finish the sentence, Karly took off running down the hallway toward the back of the house.

Erin straightened, and allowed herself a moment to really look at Zack. The cocky, confident man she'd enjoyed spending time with over the last few months was nowhere to be found. The sexy, caring guy she'd been intimate with since Thanksgiving, learning every inch of his beautiful body, was gone. Even the cheerful, caring dad who'd donned a silly costume to help out with the birthday festivities earlier in the day had disappeared.

In his place was this hard-edged guy, oozing cynicism, anger, and despair.

His frown was impressive. "Are you gonna invite me in? Or do you plan to hold both of my kids hostage," he snapped.

"I think it's best we talk out here for now," Erin said quietly, stepping onto the wide porch and closing the front door in her wake. She ignored the kidnapping innuendo and focused on the man in front of her. Who was obviously in pain.

"What, we're hiding now? So your fiancé won't overhear you talking to the jilted lover?"

"What are you talking about?"

"Leo of course. I figured he'd still be here with you. Making wedding plans."

"Leo Kensington left. Actually, he won't be staying for Christmas." There was so much more to that, but she didn't want to get into it. Not now. Not when she'd spent the last few hours consoling her daughter about the father who didn't really want her. Leo only wanted his inheritance. A convenient wife and daughter, a pre-made family, was a shortcut to getting it faster. Leo was a cheater at heart, in all things.

"I'm not staying for Christmas either."

What? What did that mean?

"You're not staying on the Cape? What about the kids?"

Zack shook his head, not meeting her eyes. "We still need to film that last episode for the spring season. Can't do that here, since it's winter, so the crew is heading to the Caribbean."

Her mouth fell open. She'd thought for sure the boy had exaggerated, or misunderstood an overheard conversation. "Bobby was right? You're leaving? Abandoning Bobby and Karly, and going back to your other life. *Your job.*"

Zack shook his head and let out a heavy sigh, still staring down at the wide planks of the wooden porch floor. "He's only half right. I'm not sure what parts of my conversation he may have heard, but I'm talking with the network about changing the focus of my show to more family-friendly adventures. This trip will not only be the final episode for the spring season, but a proof of concept for the show's new direction. *Epic Adventures, Family Edition*. I'm bringing the kids and their grandparents along for the ride."

"Oh." She was quiet for a moment, trying to decide what to say. She settled on the simple truth. "I thought we were spending the holidays together."

"Why?"

"What do you mean why?"

"Aren't you headed back to England to marry Leo?"

She took a full step back. "What?"

"I heard you two talking this afternoon. I heard him propose. I saw the ring."

"And?"

Zack made a rolling gesture with his hand, as if the rest was an obvious conclusion. "He's Hailey's father. Family is important to you."

"Family is important. But so is love." She stepped closer again, close enough to feel the heat and anger pouring off his body. "And I don't love Leo."

"Of course you do."

"No. I don't." She took another step, close enough now that she could practically feel the pounding of his heart.

"No?" Hope flickered in his eyes, the grey depths swirling.

"No, you dummy. I told you already. I love you." She went up on her toes and pressed her lips to his in a soft kiss. A promise.

Those moonstone eyes she's spent so much of her youth dreaming about, cataloging their changes in color, darkened to a molten grey that held promises of their own. But still, they seemed wary.

"Zack. I love you," she repeated. "I thought we were on the same page?"

He hesitated before speaking. "It's easier to live life on my own terms, alone, than to… take chances. Take that risk. Trust that someone will be there. That *you'll* be there tomorrow. Next year. Ten years from now. You make me want the kind of future that I never thought about before. Before you."

She closed her eyes for a brief moment, her stomach bottoming out, letting the uncertainty in his voice wash through her.

In his experience, everyone did leave.

Maybe not by choice, but he'd been on his own for a long time.

He cleared his throat. "When I heard him propose to you, I figured... well, I figured that was it."

"I said no to him. His proposal wasn't real. He doesn't love us." She kept her voice low. Even though she did the right thing by turning him down, it still hurt that Leo didn't really want her or Hailey.

Zack nodded, not meeting her eyes. "How can... how do you learn to trust that someone won't just... leave?"

"I get it. I've been there too."

He scoffed and shot her a look filled with disbelief. "You? Your family is like an army at your beck and call."

She closed her eyes again. "Zack."

"Oh. You mean Leo." Zack huffed out a breath. "Sorry. This trust thing is scary. I can admit it's scary... because I've already imagined taking that next step with you. I can't seem to picture a future without you. But it's too fast. Too soon. Too much." Zack took a step back. "I know I'm famous for leaping out of helicopters and jumping off cliffs, but somehow this seems more frightening than any of my TV adventures."

She closed the gap between them and put her arms around his waist. "I've spent the last six years playing it safe. Not taking any risks, let alone risking my heart. But Zack, you're worth the risk. I love you."

Zack planted a gentle kiss on her forehead. "You said that already."

"I'll keep saying it until you believe me. I love you, and I'm not going anywhere."

"You mean... not to England."

"That's what I mean, you big dummy. I'm staying right here."

He stared at her, the darkness in his eyes beginning to lighten. "And what if I told you I love you, too? That maybe I want to see how this whole family thing might work out?"

"Family thing?"

"You. Me. Three kids." He looked around the wide, wraparound porch. "Although it might get crowded here with your folks. You and Hailey should probably move in with us."

"So you're planning to stay in Chatham?"

He shrugged. "It's our home."

"And what about your show? And Christmas?"

"We'll have to see what the network says about the new direction of the show. In the meantime, how about coming to Turks and Caicos for the holidays with us? Your parents can come too, if you want them to."

They locked eyes for a solid minute before her wide smile answered his question.

"I thought you'd never ask."

EPILOGUE

Christmas Week
Turks & Caicos

he robin's egg blue sky nudged against the clear turquoise water of the calmest ocean Erin had ever seen. She'd lived along the Atlantic coast for almost all of her life, and although this was still technically the same ocean, she didn't recognize it one bit.

This was paradise.

Warm ocean water, white sand beaches, perfect tropical breezes, beautiful sunsets every night, friendly people everywhere they visited…

Definitely paradise.

Yesterday they'd snorkeled near the third largest coral reef in the world, Mike with his underwater camera capturing the excited reactions to the brilliantly colored schools of fish that inhabited the underwater ecosystem. Today they explored a mangrove cove in transparent kayaks – totally clear polycarbonate plastic so everything swimming by was practically in your lap! Who thought of these things?

With the crew following along in a pair of flat bottom boats filming the idyllic scene, and the trusty Mike in his own clear kayak paddled by a guide, Zack led the way, pointing out the sea turtles, brightly colored fish, and even small lemon sharks under the surface. The cameras caught his narration and the reactions from the three kids who were the new focus of the show. Bobby, Hailey, and Karly were having the best time exploring all there was for children to see and do on Turks and Caicos.

Epic Adventures, Family Edition. The "proof of concept" episode.

If Mike's enthusiasm was anything to judge by, the new direction for the show was going to be a big hit.

She glanced over at Zack, currently explaining to the kids, and by extension the future television audience, how the sea turtles swam into shallows like this in the late afternoons to eat the sea grass that grew like meadows in the clear water. Hailey was practically falling out of their kayak to listen to his story, hanging on his every word. Zack had that charisma thing going that was engaging for all ages.

A swell of emotion rose in her chest, thinking for a moment how lucky those two kids in the kayak with him were to have him as their uncle. Their guardian. Their protector.

How lucky she was to have him in her life, and more than lucky that Hailey loved him too.

But most of all, how lucky she felt to find real love. That they'd both been brave enough to take that leap of faith, trusting the other would be there. Whether it was on Cape Cod or somewhere else in the world on an adventure. Together.

In the end, they compromised for Christmas and stayed on Cape Cod with her parents, where Santa had brought brand new bicycles for all three kids. The following day, her father drove them all to Logan Airport. Agnes and Richard joined them at their stopover in Florida before they flew to Grand Turk, two sets of grandparents and three overly excited children. The Mills planned to jump on a cruise ship in a few days for a New Years trip around the Caribbean, Zack's

Christmas gift to them. Erin's parents were staying on with them, and had even participated in a few of the excursions.

At first, having his grandparents around made Bobby upset, as if he was sure Zack was giving up his role as guardian. The two had taken a long walk on the beach together that first day at the resort, and since then everything had been smooth sailing. Especially since Agnes and Richard opted out of any of the adventuring, choosing instead to stay by the resorts pool during the day and only joining them for meals. As much as Agnes had first argued about wanting to take the children to live in Florida, Erin was absolutely sure Zack made the better parent, and that Bobby and Karly were in good hands.

"Mom, they're getting too far ahead of us," Hailey complained, rousing Erin from her musings. "Even Grandma and Grandpa are ahead of us! Look! They're going closer to the mangrove trees, to the beach to see the lizards!"

"Well, we can't miss that," Erin agreed, putting more effort into her strokes. "And I think you mean iguanas, sweetie."

"Iguanas are still lizards. And pretty close to dragons." Hailey shifted, turning to face her mother. "Bobby really liked the black dragon I gave him for Christmas, didn't he? Now we both have dragons of our own."

Erin smiled. "Yes, he really did. Maybe we should have picked one out for Karly, too."

"Nah, she doesn't like dragons. Although I saw her looking at that sea turtle stuffie in the gift shop. Maybe we should buy one of those for her, especially after today."

"That's a great idea."

Hailey was still facing her, not paddling. "Mom? Is Karly like my little sister now?"

Erin stilled, laying her paddle across her lap. She ignored the fact that Zack and the other two kids had already pulled their kayak up on the shore to look at the iguanas up close. This conversation was too important to rush. "Do you want her to be?"

"I do, because that means Bobby is my brother. I always wanted a brother."

Her eyes hot with sudden tears, Erin nodded. "I didn't know that." She swallowed the emotions clogging her throat. "I'm sorry things didn't work out with your father. With Leo."

Hailey shrugged, her blue eyes locked with Erin's. "That's okay. He doesn't really love us. Not like Zack does."

Out of the mouths of babes. All Erin could do was nod in agreement.

LATER THAT NIGHT, while Richard and Tom watched football at the resort's sports bar, and Agnes and Maureen tucked three exhausted children into bed in the shared villa, Zack and Erin took some time alone to stroll hand in hand along the white sand beach. The setting sun turned the entire sky into a blaze of reds and oranges, the purples of twilight slowly edging out the brighter colors as darkness fell.

Scattered along the beach at intervals were tiki torches, some with groupings of lounge chairs and people with cocktails in hand, a few with empty tables set with white tablecloths for couples to enjoy a romantic dinner under the stars.

A beautiful night. A gorgeous setting. Perfect for romance.

She pushed down the nerves threatening to keep her silent, and cleared her throat. "Hey, I wanted to talk with you about something Hailey said today."

"Oh yeah? What's that?"

Zack's warm gaze and easy smile eased the tension that had been building inside her since the kayaking trip.

"She asked if she could consider Karly and Bobby as siblings now that we're officially dating."

"Interesting. And what did you say?" Zack's eyes held hers, not showing any of the panic she'd expected to see.

"I didn't know how to answer her, not really. But it made me think." She pulled him to a stop on the sand. "We talked before about Hailey and I moving in with you."

He took both of her hands and held them together in his. "You never really gave me an answer about that."

She huffed out a laugh even as she felt her cheeks start to burn.

166

Thankfully it was too dark now for him to see her blush. "I know it sounds archaic, but since I teach kindergarten, it's not a good idea. I'm not sure the PTA or the school board would approve of us *living in sin*, as they say. I'd have to check the fine print of my contract, but it's probably a bad idea to test them."

He nodded, his smile still warm. "That's what I figured."

She swallowed. "Which is why I think it might be a good idea to get married."

"Erin Leigh Brannigan. Are you proposing to me?"

She nodded slowly, unsure how to interpret his calm reaction. Or when he'd figured out her middle name. "I love you. You love me. We both love those kids. I think we make sense. We could be a real family."

He pulled her closer and wrapped his arms around her, holding her tight. She buried her face against his chest, feeling the steady drumbeat of his heart against her cheek, waiting for his answer. Long moments that felt like an eternity slowly passed, until he finally pulled away, and took her hands again.

"I'll say yes if you say yes."

"What?" Confusion filled her. "What do you mean?"

Still holding both hands, he dragged her over to one of the small tables set for dinner, awash with torchlight and romance. A scattering of rose petals covered the tablecloth, a single rose in a vase atop one of the place settings, with a ring box next to it. Zack grabbed the velvet box and dropped to both knees in the sand next to the table.

"I love you, Erin. I want to be a real family with you, and with Hailey, and with Bobby and Karly. But most important, I love you. Marry me."

A surprised laugh escaped her. "Are you asking me or telling me?"

"Well, you 're the one who told me it would be a good idea."

She thought back to her own botched proposal and laughed. "Yeah, I guess I did."

"So, what do you think?" He opened the box and offered it to her. Nestled inside, a square cut aquamarine surrounded by a halo of tiny diamonds sparkled in the torchlight, the blue the same color as the ocean had been earlier in the day.

Her breath caught in her throat. "Oh Zack, it's gorgeous."

"Not as gorgeous as you," he said, finally getting up from his knees. He took the ring from the box and slipped it on her left hand. "So. Will you marry me?"

"Absolutely!" For a moment, she held her hand up high, admiring the way the ring sparkled in the moonlight, and even more, the way it made her feel. Loved. Truly loved.

She threw both arms around his neck, pulling his face toward hers for a kiss, tongues sliding together in a sensuous dance. More than a kiss, it felt like a promise.

A promise of family. Of forever.

The End

BONUS RECIPES

Sometimes when I'm reading a story that has food involved, I start to obsess and wonder about the recipes. If you were wondering about Hailey's cookies or Aunt Barbara's famous Bundt cake, or making chocolate chip pancakes, or even how to make pudding in a bag... I thought I'd share these secrets with you.

Because sometimes you just need chocolate.

And yes, these are all very simple recipes that are easy enough for a kindergartener to help whip up for the holidays. Or any time you need a little chocolate in your life.

HAILEY'S FAMOUS CHOCOLATE CHIP COOKIES

Ingredients:

- 2 sticks of butter
- 1 cup white sugar
- ¾ cup brown sugar
- 1 teaspoon vanilla extract
- 2 eggs
- 2 1/3 cups flour
- 1 teaspoon baking soda
- 1 teaspoon salt
- 2 ½ cups chocolate chips

Directions:

Preheat oven to 375 degrees.
Cream butter and sugars together.
Add vanilla and eggs; stir until smooth.
Add flour, baking soda, and salt; stir until smooth.
Add chocolate chips; stir until evenly distributed through dough
Drop onto cookie sheets 2 inches apart.
Bake 8-10 minutes until brown at edges and cooked through.
Let cool on wire rack.

AUNT BARBARA'S CHOCOLATE BUNDT CAKE

Ingredients:

- 1 box Devil's Food cake mix
- 1 small box instant chocolate pudding
- 1 cup brewed coffee
- 4 eggs
- 1 cup sour cream
- ½ cup vegetable oil
- 2 cups chocolate chips

Directions:

Preheat oven to 350 degrees.
Combine all ingredients except chocolate chips.
Blend with mixer on low speed.
Beat with mixture on medium speed for 2 minutes.
Fold in chocolate chips with wooden spoon.
Pour into greased and floured Bundt pan.
Bake 55-60 minutes until toothpick comes out clean.
Let cool completely. Dust with powdered sugar right before serving.

Pro Tip: Use oil to grease Bundt pan; use a little of the cake mix instead of flour to coat sides.

CHOCOLATE CHIP GRIDDLE PANCAKES (WITHOUT A MIX)

Ingredients:

- 1 ¼ cups flour
- 2 Tablespoons white sugar
- 2 teaspoons baking powder
- ½ teaspoon salt
- 1 egg, beaten
- 1 cup milk (whole, 2%, soy, or almond milk all work fine)
- 1 Tablespoon olive oil
- Mini chocolate chips (mini work best, but regular chips will do in a pinch)

Directions:

Stir together flour, sugar, baking powder, and salt. In separate bowl, combine egg, milk, and oil. Add wet ingredients into dry, stirring together until blended.

Pour ¼ cup batter onto hot, lightly greased griddle (or skillet if you don't have a pancake griddle) for each pancake. Sprinkle with mini chips. When pancakes have a bubbly surface and slightly dry edges, flip to cook side with chips. Cook until golden brown.

Serve with maple syrup and/or whipped cream.

CHOCOLATE PUDDING-IN-A-BAG

Ingredients:

- Instant Chocolate Pudding Mix (needs to be instant)
- Cold Whole milk (works best with whole milk)
- Zip-top plastic bag(s)

Directions:

Measure 2 Tablespoons of pudding mix into bag. Add ½ cup of milk. Carefully seal bag, making sure to get all the air bubbles out. Squish bag to mix the ingredients tougher, and keep squishing until pudding thickens. Cut off one bottom corner of bag to squeeze pudding out, straight into your mouth.

ACKNOWLEDGMENTS

As I always say, very few authors ever reach "the end" without plenty of help. I need to say thank you to my family, friends, and coworkers (both online and in real life) who fill my world with laughter, love, and support. And big hugs to my readers who give me feedback and encouragement through emails, letters, and especially by leaving reviews.

Huge shoutouts to my beta readers, especially Deb and Andy, for helping fine tune the story, to Claire for helping with the book description, and to Michele for creating such a fun book cover! A Big Thank You also goes out Tamara Ferguson for the invitation to her 2024 Christmas anthology of new works and the original prompt that kicked off the story. And to Dorothy Cohen for being a Scout leader with me all those years ago, brave enough to teach fifteen little kids how to make pudding in a bag. And good enough help clean up afterwards.

If you enjoyed this Cape Cod Christmas story, check out some of my other Cape Cod romances – including *Once Upon a Christmas Cookie* (available in paperback as well as Kindle), which incorporates and details a few of Zack and Erin's favorite Christmas traditions on the Cape that were touched on in this story. Christmas on Cape Cod is truly magical. (There's a sneak peek included with this book!)

Please consider leaving a review on Amazon or Goodreads (or both!) Each and every review is important, helping other readers discover my books. Reviews don't have to be book reports – merely a few sentences about whether you liked a book and why. Reviews make all the difference to someone else trying to make a decision. (And to me! I love reviews!) Thanks in advance for sharing your opinions.

MORE ROMANCE FROM KATIE O'SULLIVAN

Ghost in the Machine

Once Upon a Christmas Cookie

Breaking the Rules

Bending the Rules

Changing the Rules

Cape Cod Dating Rules – the complete *Rules* series paperback

Quinn's Resolution

Brendan's Christmas Surprise

Ed's Blind Date Dilemma

My Everyday Hero: Logan

Battling Benjamin

Matt's Mystic Connection

From The Wild Rose Press:

My Kind of Crazy

Crazy About You

Ghosts Don't Lie

Say Yes (a Candy Hearts Romance)

Be My Hero (Candy Hearts Series Box Set)

EXCERPT FROM ONCE UPON A CHRISTMAS COOKIE

PUBLISHED 2022 FROM WINDMILL POINT
PUBLISHING

Matt Jamieson is done with casual hookups, but his playboy reputation isn't easy to shake off. Volunteering with his niece's scout troop is the ticket to showing everyone he's ready to settle down, but the fiery redhead who pushes all his buttons is an obstacle he didn't anticipate.

Chelsea Greene never meant to move back to Cape Cod. Thanks to grad school loans and a mountain of debt from her cheating ex, she's once again sleeping in her childhood bed. But when the holidays and the annual open house competition roll around, her mom asks for a favor she can't refuse.

All Chelsea needs to do is go on a date with the obnoxious guy from the craft fair to get the cookie recipe her mother needs. But when one date turns into two, and then three... can they still blame it on the Snickerdoodles? Or is there a pinch of holiday magic in that secret recipe?

CHAPTER 1

*T*he corner of Matt Jamieson's mouth ticked up as she made yet another outrageous promise.

"C'mon, Matt. Say yes and I'll love you forever!"

He couldn't help but smirk. He'd heard that desperation at least a million times over the course of his lifetime, all twenty-six years of it, and it never got old. He enjoyed doing favors for others, but more importantly, he loved to be "loved" – yeah, he could admit he was a people pleaser, and so what? He liked making people happy. Liked to see them smile and know he was the reason.

Of course, he'd heard that particular phrase from this particular woman standing in front of him more often than from anyone else.

"Maureen, I'm your baby brother. You have to love me, and you really ought to get some new lines."

But staring into her deep blue eyes, a mirror image to his own, he felt himself relenting even before she formulated the next plea. He knew he was going to say yes, but still wanted to make her work for it. That's what little brothers were best at, right? Annoying older siblings. At least he'd made sure that was true in the Jamieson house-hold. So what if there were only the two of them? Their mom probably would've had a bunch more kids if their dad had lived longer.

Maureen doubled down on her pleading, her words now tumbling over each other in a fast-paced frenzy, even as she bustled around the kitchen, pulling two trays of cookies from one of the ovens and shoving two more in their place before resetting the timer. "I swear, I never would've volunteered if I knew about this order, but it came in at the last minute from the Chamber of Commerce when their other baker fell through, and this could really boost holiday sales for the bakery. Can you picture it? Can't you see it in your head? My logo on every bag of cookies that Santa hands out at tomorrow's town hall event." She swiped one flour-covered hand down the front of her apron, as if to highlight the bakery's logo.

The Rolling Pin. The 1950s-looking logo went with the retro feel Maureen had out front in the public part of the shop, where he could hear one of the local high schoolers who worked the counter chatting it up with a customer. Blue and white checked curtains and table-cloths, kitschy signs lining the wall around the price menu, and a large brass baker's rack filled with old fashioned mixers, wooden rolling pins, and muffin tins. The vibe was totally an old fashioned, home-baked-goodness kind of feeling. Which fit in with the rest of the Harwich Center shops rather well, given the eclectic mix of retailers and eating establishments, not one of them part of a chain or larger conglomerate.

Before Maureen moved back to Cape Cod, this former diner sat empty for a handful of years, as if waiting for the right person to breathe life into it. Despite the tragedy that brought her home, Maureen plowed ahead and poured her entire focus into making her new venture a success. While the shop hadn't been able to open in time to take advantage of the summer tourist season, the locals stepped up to support one of their own when tragic tides returned her to their shore. Many of their mother's friends, neighbors, and former coworkers stopped in on a regular basis to buy baked goods, keeping Maureen's new dream afloat until the return of tourist season.

Here in the back room of the small shop, everything was all stain-less steel counters and industrial-size mixers surrounded by bright white walls and tiled floors. The warmth from the busy ovens and the comforting scent of cinnamon swirled through the air, surrounding him, wrapping around him like a cozy blanket. A pair of commercial-grade convection double ovens that Matt helped her pick out at the appliance center off-Cape counted down the minutes before the next batches of cookies would be ready. Matt salivated at the thought of all that sugary perfection.

"Ple-e-e-ease?" Maureen drew out the word forever, her pleading tone refocusing his attention on the conversation at hand.

"You realize this is my Friday night we're talking about, don't you?" And Matt had plans. Big plans. Well, okay, maybe not really all that big. More like, he had a plan to make a plan. He still needed to return Derrick's call about meeting up. His friend left a message earlier about a pair of twins and a dire need for Matt to play the part of wingman. Blondes who were only in Chatham for the weekend and looking for, as Derrick described it, the "full Cape Cod experience."

The old Matt would've jumped right on that, calling his buddy immediately to make that plan a reality. No brainer. After a painful break with his college sweetheart, he spent month after month hooking up with every woman who smiled his way. He'd spent way too much time trying to drown the memories of Lorraine and his own starry-eyed foolishness... trying to fill the emptiness she left in her wake when she'd publicly yanked out his heart and stomped all over it.

In the end, it was simple. They wanted different things out of life. Despite the fact that they attended the same college, and the same architectural degree program, her ideal life was in Manhattan helping build brand spanking new skyscrapers. His dream was to live here on Cape Cod, doing restoration work on landmark buildings and historic sea captain homes. While they say opposite attract, having opposite life goals was apparently a recipe for disaster. Who knew?

Lorraine did.

She told him in no uncertain terms that she would never be happy living anywhere outside of a major city... he just wished she'd mentioned it before he'd gone and spent so much on the stupid ring.

Before he bent one knee the night before their graduation ceremony. In front of all their friends.

Her pitying tone echoed in the back of Matt's head even now, two years later. *"I can't marry you, Matt. I thought you understood. I'm going back to New York to work at my father's firm."*

"I'll move to New York with you," he offered. He hated big cities, but he loved Lorraine.

She shook her head. "It would never work long term. What we had was fine for college, but Matt, you must see it too. I want more out of life than you will ever be able to give me. You're just not a guy to get serious with."

And that was the part that stung the most. That he wasn't enough. That he would never be enough for someone like Lorraine.

He'd spent the better part of the last few years drowning his unwanted feelings in work, along with a non-stop parade of willing women. Tourists exactly like the blond twins Derrick mentioned in his text – women who knew the score and were just looking for a good time. One and done, because his heart was no longer part of the equation.

But then the accident that took Maureen's husband in September – and subsequently brought her home – gave Matt some much needed perspective. Lorraine's departure hadn't been the end of life, not like how Maureen's world collapsed. Shot during a robbery, Joe's death left her with an empty bed, a small child, and a place of business she couldn't even walk into without bursting into uncontrollable tears. She'd sold their small restaurant and house on Long Island, and moved back home to Cape Cod.

Over the last several months he spent most of his time helping his sister rather than chasing blondes. He'd do anything to help his big sister make a go of her new business, so he knew he was going to say yes to her in the end. Being Santa's cookie baker was too good an opportunity to pass up, no matter what the circumstances. She was right – it would give the bakery some much needed visibility for the slow winter months to come.

But he still enjoyed making her grovel. Just a little. Again, only doing his duty as an annoying little brother.

"Please, Matt, pretty please? I even baked an extra batch of my special Snickerdoodles for the girls to sell at their craft table. I only signed up for a two-hour shift, so you'll still be able to go out with your buddies and pick up girls, or whatever you plan to do later tonight."

"I don't always pick up girls," Matt said defensively.

Maureen rolled her eyes at his statement but didn't contradict him. "Please do this for me? For Lilly?"

He took the bag and glanced inside, almost drooling at the sight of all those plastic sandwich baggies, each containing a trio of cookies. Christmas cookies were always his favorite part of the holiday season, and he'd quickly become addicted to his sister's new Snickerdoodle recipe, one of the shop's signature cookies for the winter season. He knew Maureen used his grandmother's original recipe, the one they'd baked with Nonna when they were kids, but his sister had changed it a little, adding a pinch of sea salt and a dash of freshly ground nutmeg along with the cinnamon sugar dusting the tops of the cookies, making them even more irresistible.

He glanced at Maureen and stroked a hand through his beard, narrowing his eyes, as if this were a serious negotiation. As if he hadn't already decided to help her out. "Do I get to keep the leftover cookies?"

"Absolutely." She grinned with obvious relief. "You know you really are a good guy, Matt. Even if you like to give me a hard time."

"Jeez, Maureen, don't go spreading crazy rumors like that around Harwich. Next thing you know everyone's gonna want me to do favors for them." He crossed his arms over his chest, pretending to be offended.

She made a shoo-ing motion with both hands. "Get out of here. Pick up Lilly and go rock that craft fair."

"You know we will." He hefted the bag of cookies and gave her a crooked smile. "But don't be late picking her up afterward. I've got a hot date waiting over in Chatham."

Maureen waved him off with a laugh. "What else is new? You always have a hot date waiting."

"Are you calling me predictable?"

"Nope." She smiled. "Predictable isn't the word I was thinking of. Casanova? Don Juan? Lothario? Something more along those lines."

Matt smiled back and waved his goodbyes as he let himself out the back door into the parking lot. So what if Maureen thought he was a player? He might never be the guy someone wanted to get serious with, but he knew he could show them a good time.

On his way to his truck, he pulled out his phone and texted Derrick about his change of plans, saying he had to help out his sister and niece before he could head over to Chatham.

His buddy's return text was practically instantaneous. **What time can you get here? These girls are ready and willing.**

Matt smirked at the string of emojis that popped up next – two hotdogs and two tacos, followed by two peaches and two eggplants. As if he didn't understand what Derrick meant by *ready and willing*.

I'll meet you at 8:30. 9 at the latest, he texted back. A thumbs up emoji popped up and Matt pocketed his phone.

He might never be anyone's *Mr. Right*, but he could totally be their *Mr. Right Now*.

CHAPTER 2

*T*raffic slowed when Matt got to the edge of downtown Harwich Port, thousands upon thousands of white lights creating a glow over the entire area. Between the long line of cars and the pedestrians spilling off the sidewalks, he felt like he'd been time warped back to the height of summer, even though all of the visitors now wore puffy jackets and long pants instead of tank tops and shorts.

The Town of Harwich always held their annual Holiday Stroll on the first Friday in December, kicking off the official holiday count-down on Cape Cod. Every small town on the Cape had their own version of a stroll, designed to help the local brick-and-mortar shops compete against the big box stores and online merchants. Every weekend was filled with holiday-themed events in towns up and down the coast, right through the big New Year's Eve First Night cele-bration on the streets of downtown Chatham.

Twenty minutes of stop and start traffic later, Matt finally turned down a side street. Like a Christmas miracle, he found an empty parking spot behind the Old Church, which seemed to glow from the inside with otherworldly light, stained glass windows shooting bright colors into the darkened parking lot. Their destination was actually the adjacent church hall, a no-nonsense white clapboard building that was well over a hundred years old. One of Matt's first jobs after graduation had been on the team of restoration woodworkers involved in the lengthy project of bringing the church and its outbuildings up to code and ready for the next hundred years.

"Uncle Matt, are you dropping me off? Or are you gonna stay and help?" Lilly's high voice piped up from the back seat.

He caught her eyes in the rearview mirror. "Of course I'm going to stay with you, Lilly-pad. Your mom signed me up to help sell stuff with you at the stroll tonight." He got out of the car and helped his niece unbuckle her car seat. "Why are you so worried?"

She shrugged and pushed her long blond braids behind her back. "None of my friends are going to be helping tonight."

"Aren't all the girls in the troop your friends?" Matt wasn't exactly sure how scouting worked, but he was pretty sure being "a friend to every scout" was on one of those patches on her vest. Or maybe it was left over from her old troop in New York.

Her little face screwed up into a sort of frown. "Kind of? But I don't know them too well yet. The girls who signed up for tonight are all third graders. So, you know, they're old."

Lilly and her mother came to Cape Cod in September, moving back into the house Matt and Maureen grew up in. Maureen used the money from the sale of her New York house and restaurant to purchase her shop. Cooking had been her husband's thing. Maureen was the baker in the family, so it made more sense for her to open a bakery. His seven-year-old niece seemed to take the transition to a new town and new school in stride, but her comment made Matt wonder if she was doing as well as everyone thought.

He forced a smile onto his face, ignoring the turn of his thoughts and responding to her words. "Well, that's what events like this are for, right? Getting to know each other better. But don't you worry. I'll be right by your side."

"Thanks, Uncle Matt."

"Although, you're going to have to fill me in on what exactly we're selling."

"Ornaments. We made a bunch of different ones at our last troop meeting." Holding firmly onto his hand, she hopped down from his truck onto the pavement. "I'll show you which ones I made, in case you want one for your Christmas tree."

"Of course I want one, silly girl. Maybe more than one. First let me grab the cookies your mom sent and then we can go inside."

Lilly tugged his arm, a giant frown on her face. "Uncle Matt, we're not allowed to sell cookies! The church ladies have a special bake sale tonight. Ornaments only, my leaders told us."

Matt considered leaving the cookies in the car to keep for himself. His sister's Snickerdoodles were the best cookies he'd ever tasted, hands down. But she'd sent them for the fundraiser. "How about instead of selling them, we give them away to customers as a bonus?"

Lilly's frown disappeared. "That sounds awesome!" She grabbed his hand and tugged him toward the door.

THE OLD CHURCH Hall buzzed with activity. Classic holiday tunes played in the background while shoppers meandered between the tables. Various nonprofit organizations displayed handmade holiday crafts, while signs posted along the walls touted the different charities and groups being represented. At the far end of the hall loomed a large stage, where the Ladies' Auxiliary had set up their holiday bake sale event. Matt spotted the scout table, where three girls dressed in vests similar to Lilly's were having what looked like a heated debate. A frazzled woman, totally ignoring any would-be shoppers, was trying to break up the escalating argument.

Matt stepped up and rapped his knuckles on the table, immediately grabbing the attention of the woman and all three girls, the fight seemingly forgotten.

"Can we help you?" The woman batted her eyelashes at Matt, trying for a smile and settling for a half-grimace when one of the girls shoved the other, who fell on the floor and started to yell again.

"Hey, are you Amanda Baker?"

The woman did a fast double take, before eyeing him from head to toe with a slow perusal that made him feel a little dirty in the process. Fire engine red lips drew into a wide, knowing smile. "Matthew Jamieson! My oh my, I haven't seen you since high school!" Her eyes did another languid crawl over his body, totally ignoring the fighting girls at her back.

"Hi...?" Matt couldn't place the woman to save his life. How did she know his name?

"I heard you and Derrick Daniels have been hanging out together again? The Dynamic Duo back in action, like old times?"

Her wink sent a chill down his spine, his skin prickling from that hungry gaze. He felt uncomfortable that he couldn't pick this woman out of a lineup when she obviously remembered not only him but his best friend. From high school. Amanda Baker... Amanda Baker... the only Amanda he remembered was Amanda Greenlaw, who his friend Derrick took to prom because it was rumored she gave the best hummers on the cheer squad. The following Monday at school, Derrick told him she'd offered to have a threesome, but that he couldn't track Matt down in time.

Matt squinted. Could this be her? Should he ask or would that be insulting? He decided to skip the confirmation of her identity – it wasn't like he wanted to take her up on the obvious offer her eyes were making. Instead, he kept it simple and answered just the question she asked.

"Uh, yeah, so, Derrick and I are still friends."

"Interesting. I haven't thought about *One-and-Done* Daniels in quite a few years. Although, he and I had more than the usual *one*, if you know what I mean," Amanda purred, ignoring the kids entirely. "I'd love to get reacquainted with an old friend, now that I'm single again." Her tongue did a slow glide across her lower lip.

Putting a hand on Lilly's shoulder, Matt tugged her little body tight against his side like a shield against further trips down memory lane. As if he should need to remind her that there were children present and listening to every word of the conversation. This was going to be an excruciating two hours if this woman spent the whole time winking and making suggestive remarks. "I'm here with Lilly to help out. Are you all the six to eight o'clock shift?"

Amanda's mascara-caked eyes widened and her lascivious smile faltered as she took in the little girl at his side. She recalibrated quickly. "Wait, you're my replacement? Oh thank the heavens!" Her tone shifted from practically purring to full-on *Mom-at-the-end-of-her-rope*.

"Replacement?" Matt frowned.

"We've been here since set-up at four and I've had about as much Christmas music and whining girls as I can stomach for one night." She turned back to the trio of scouts still arguing behind the table. "Grace and Heather, grab your coats and we're out of here."

The third girl raised her hand. "What about me, Mrs. Baker?"

"Sarah, you need to stay here with Mr. Jamieson until a parent comes to pick you up."

The girl pouted for half a second before she squealed and pointed across the crowded hall. "I see Mom over at the cookie table. Can I go now, please?" She grabbed her coat and sprinted off without waiting for an answer.

Faster than he would've thought possible, Amanda and the two remaining girls donned their coats and moved out from behind the table.

Matt's eyes widened. "Wait, that's it? Lilly and I are standing here alone? I thought there were other scouts signed up to sell crafts with us?"

"If they show up." Amanda wound a colorful knit scarf around her neck. "There was supposed to be another mom and three more girls to help us schlepp all this stuff from my car into the hall for set up. But they never showed. If no one comes to help you on this shift, the last group of scouts should arrive at eight. They'll be the ones to pack it up again, since Karen McClure is one of the troop leaders. She was a grade above us in school, so you might not remember her."

That's a better-than-good possibility, since I barely remember you. Matt kept the thought to himself, asking the more pertinent question at hand. "How long does this event last?"

"From five until ten. But we were here at four to set up, so our two hours are done. See you around town." She paused to wink at him, giving her bottom lip once last swipe of the tongue. "And let your friend Derrick know I asked after him. Tell him to call me sometime."

The two other girls waved at Lilly as they walked away, never bothering to say hello or goodbye. They soon blended into the crowd, leaving him alone with his niece and a table full of crafts to sell. At least he wouldn't have to spend the next two hours fending off unwanted advances. And Lilly wouldn't have to deal with being ignored by the older girls.

Matt squeezed Lilly's shoulder. "Looks like it's just you and me, kiddo."

"Don't worry, Uncle Matt. We practiced being good salespeople at our meeting last week." She dragged him behind the craft table and shrugged off her winter coat, dropping it to the floor and kicking it to the side against the wall.

"Oh yeah? What did you learn?" He removed his own leather jacket and folded it in half, looking for a place to set it down where it wouldn't get trampled. As he knelt to put his coat atop a plastic bin under the table, he got an up close look at the ornaments the girls crafted. He had one word for them all.

Ugly.

Yet another thought to keep to himself.

Painted seashells with yarn loops for hangers, macaroni angels covered in glitter and globs of dried glue, jingle bells made from egg cartons and pipe cleaners, snowflakes cut from glittery paper and dusted with cinnamon, everything covered in sequins and more glitter... sure, he knew his mother's tree held similar creations from when he and Maureen were young, but would anyone spend money on ugly ornaments crafted by someone else's kids?

"Lilly, how much is the troop charging for these... creations? I don't see a price list."

"Everything is one dollar, Uncle Matt, except the painted scallop shells are two for a dollar." Lilly pointed at a Christmas wrapped box sitting on the corner of the table. "That box is for donations. I heard one of the leaders say they usually make more from donations than from sales."

Not a big surprise. Matt kept that thought to himself too.

"Uncle Matt, what did Mrs. Baker mean by *One-and-Done*? I thought Mr. Daniels's first name was Derrick?"

Matt winced. "You're right, Lilly-pad. His real name is Derrick. That was his nickname back in high school." When his friend would date a girl just long enough to get her to sleep with him, and then dump her.

"That's a silly nickname," Lilly proclaimed, with the authority only a small child could bring to the conversation.

Before she could continue down that line of questioning, Matt changed the subject. "What is the troop raising money for? A camping trip?"

Lilly scrunched up her face and tapped a finger against her chin, Derrick's nickname and Mrs. Baker forgotten. "I think they said whatever we earn we'll spend to buy wood. We're going to build new birdhouses for one of the conservation meadows in town to earn a wildlife conservation badge. Hey! Maybe you could come to the meeting and help us build them!"

He eyed the ornaments again. If these were any indication, Lilly's troop leaders would need all the help they could get. "Sure thing, Lilly-pad. It's for a good cause. I'll talk to your leader when she gets here at eight." With his contractor discount, he could get them a good price on the wood too, which they would definitely need if sales of ornaments were supposed to pay for the materials. Back in his own scouting days, his troop had installed some of the first bird boxes at Thompson's Field, one of the larger conservation properties in town. He was deep in his thoughts on birdhouse building when Lilly tugged his arm.

"Uncle Matt, I want you to meet my best friend Sharon."

Across the table, a girl who looked to be Lilly's age smiled at him, showing a gap where her two front teeth should've been. Behind her stood a couple who could only be her parents, since the girl looked like a mini-me of her mother.

The father reached a hand across the table. "Josh Hornbill. Sharon talks non-stop about your daughter Lilly."

"Niece," Matt corrected. "My sister Maureen had to work tonight so I volunteered to help."

"That's sweet of you." The woman cocked her head and smiled. "I'm Sharon's mom, Susan. Hey, do you mind if we borrow Lilly for a little while? We're going to stand in line to see Santa at the Information Center, and go on the," Susan made finger quotes, "*sleigh ride* around the block. Sharon thought it would be more fun with a friend."

"Oh please, Uncle Matt?" Lilly tugged his arm again, her upturned face shining with obvious excitement. "The other girls should be here soon to help you, and I'll be back really quick. Quick like a bunny. I promise! Ple-e-e-ease… can I go with Sharon?"

Matt wondered how his sister ever said no to her daughter, when the little girl could beg as well as Maureen. He heaved a sigh before chuckling, and exchanged cell numbers with Susan before he helped Lilly shrug back into her winter coat.

The girls waved good-bye as they skipped out of the church hall hand in hand.

Matt surveyed the crowded hall, alone behind the table of uber-ugly crafts and contraband cookies. Shoppers walked between the tables, chattering amongst themselves, not sparing a glance at the scout table, no matter how noble the cause.

He inhaled a long breath and blew it out slowly.

This is going to be a long night.

CHAPTER 3

This is going to be a long night.

Chelsea Greene maneuvered her car down the crowded street, avoiding the pedestrians spilling off the sidewalks and darting through the stop-and-start traffic. Which wouldn't have been nearly as nerve-wracking without the constant stream of commentary from her mother, presently ensconced in the passenger seat and blasting out snarky opinions every few minutes.

"Watch out for the group of teens with the Santa hats! They're about to jaywalk… and yes, there they go crossing the street in the middle of the block, right through all this traffic. Don't they know how to use the crosswalks? What are they teaching kids in school these days?" Martha Greene huffed with annoyance. "Why don't young people learn to obey traffic rules?"

"Mom, it's all good. I'm sure they're just excited for the start of the holiday season." Chelsea tried to keep her voice even and calm, using the same tone that worked so well with nervous dogs in her veterinary office. As low-man on the totem pole at her clinic, she got saddled with most of the routine wellness appointments as well as the administering of annual shots, so she had a lot of recent experience with nervous animals.

And moving home after grad school had given her lots of recent experience dealing with her overbearing mother.

"They still need to pay more attention to traffic," her mother said with a frown, not willing to let go of her argument.

"Traffic? Mom, our top speed has been two miles an hour since we got to the edge of Harwich Port. Are you absolutely sure we need to be here for this?"

While there were plenty of holiday events around the Cape for adults, this particular Friday night stroll was mostly for families and kids welcoming Santa. Every year, the town decorated the tourist information center on Main Street like Santa's workshop and lines of children snaked out the door on the weekends waiting for their chance to sit on the big man's lap and whisper their wishes in his ear. She remembered it fondly from her own childhood, but now? After ten hours on her feet at work, Harwich Port seemed more like a crowded nightmare than a winter wonderland.

"Chelsea, I explained all this to you in detail last night. I need to find a new cookie recipe before next weekend. That sneaky Hilda Nickerson got the judges to add the new nut-free rule at the last minute. My famous Raspberry Linzer cookies are no longer eligible to be included at the event, and you remember how close we were to winning the trophy last year. Hilda knew it too, that's for sure." Her mother grumbled that last part under her breath.

"You have to admit there *are* a lot of people in the world with nut allergies," Chelsea reminded her. It was an argument Chelsea knew she would lose, like every other time the topic arose since Thanksgiving.

Martha let out a derisive snort. "That's why we labeled them. Besides, Hilda isn't worried about anyone's health but her own. She is worried that her gingerbread won't garner first place in this year's competition."

"Mom, it's a friendly competition to raise money for the local library. It's not life or death. It's a little gold statue or whatever. Certainly not something to get this worked up about."

"Yes, but it's my turn. I *deserve* that prize." Martha shook her head dismissively. "If they made the rule change earlier, we would've had more time to investigate alternatives. Now we have less than a week to find a new cookie recipe and bake the hundreds of cookies we'll need for the event."

Chelsea rolled her eyes at her mother's use of the word "we." When it came to baking the cookies and decorating the house for the holidays, her mother was very inclusive in sharing the work and delegating tasks. When it came to winning the trophy, it was all Mom's.

The Captain Nathaniel Greene house in the Bass River neighborhood of Dennis had been in her father's family for generations, listed on the registry of historic Cape Cod homes. Chelsea was twelve the first time her parents participated in their local library's annual fundraiser, a historic house tour nicknamed the "Holiday Cookie Stroll."

Participants bought tickets ahead of time, and received a map and empty goodie bag when they checked in at the library, along with a scoring sheet. At each stop along the way, visitors walked through the historic sea captain homes, got their score sheet stamped and received a plastic baggie containing the home's signature cookies. The event sold out every year. Even though the library capped ticket sales at 250, the $35 a pop with very little overhead for the library – because really, how much could it cost to print those booklets and buy a little gold statue? - netted a tidy profit for their building maintenance fund.

Chelsea turned left out of Main Street's stop and go traffic and onto Elmwood to look for a parking spot. The sooner she got her mother to the Old Church, the sooner she could get home and put her feet up. Slipping into a newly vacated space along the side of the road, Chelsea ignored her mother's chatter as she gathered her purse from the back seat and wound her favorite blue scarf around her neck.

When she graduated from vet school, she never pictured herself spending a Friday night searching for new cookie recipes with her mother. But moving back home temporarily allowed her to save money and pay off her college debt, a decision made even easier after her ex-boyfriend used her credit cards to finance his move to the West

Coast, taking the vet tech he'd been screwing along for the trip and leaving Chelsea – and her credit rating – in the dust.

At one point, she actually thought Dillon was her Mr. Right. That they were going to get married and live happily ever after. What a joke. She learned the hard way that *happily ever afters* only existed in fairy tales and romance novels.

But for all the bad reasons that brought her back to Cape Cod, there were enough good things to keep her going, at least for the time being. Her job was great. For a small-town veterinary clinic, Harwich Animal Hospital boasted state of the art equipment and techniques. Jonathan Reynolds, the head vet, moved to the Cape from San Francisco a few years back, bringing all kinds of new ideas with him, enlivening his uncle's fifty year old practice. It was sheer luck that Dr. Reynolds, senior retired the year before, leaving an opening she was only too happy to step into. Perfect timing for Chelsea to regroup, pay off her debts, and get her life back on track before she moved on to her next adventure.

Hopefully somewhere far, far away – where she didn't live under the same roof as Martha Greene.

She loved her mother. She really did. But Martha's competitive nature had always grated on Chelsea, pushing her daughter to be the best at everything she did.

Why aren't you valedictorian, Chelsea? Salutatorian is another word for second best.

Why Cornell and not Harvard, Chelsea? Afraid you would crack under the pressure?

Why an animal doctor and not a real doctor, Chelsea?

Martha's current obsession with winning some stupid trophy only served as a reminder why Chelsea moved several hours away in the first place. *Maybe I need to adjust my timeline*, Chelsea decided. *One holiday season with Mom may be more than I can handle.*

She inhaled a deep breath and blew it out slowly, trying one of the stress reduction techniques the therapist taught her in college, running through her five senses to ground herself. *One, the feel of the soft fleece scarf around her neck. Two, the salty scent of the wind off the ocean that lay two blocks over from Main Street. Three, the twinkle of stars in the inky night sky being slowly blotted out by incoming clouds.*

"Chelsea, stop dawdling on the sidewalk!"

Four, the grate of her mother's voice in her eardrums. And five, the taste of the chardonnay she was going to need to blot the next few hours out of her memory.

Maybe not quite what the therapist had in mind, but hey. Whatever worked.

They headed up the street toward the bright lights and cheery sounds of Main Street and Chelsea ventured a question. "Tell me again why you think you'll find a new recipe at this church thing?"

Martha huffed. "I told you this before. Were you not listening to me? The ladies' group at Old Church puts out a new holiday cookbook every few years, and those old women are known as fabulous bakers. The best on Cape Cod. If I'm going to find a crowd-pleasing cookie in the short timeframe I have left, this is really my only shot."

"And why are you convinced these might be award winning recipes?"

"Where do you think I got the Linzer cookie recipe from? I may not have won the damn Holiday Cookie Stroll trophy yet, but I've certainly won other local competitions."

Chelsea crinkled her nose at her mother's declaration. "You always said those cookies were from an old family recipe."

"I never said it was *our* family. Now hurry up. They have samples of all the cookbook favorites for sale, so we can figure out which recipe will be my winner." She wrapped her hand around Chelsea's elbow, pulling her along as if she were still a child.

Chelsea bit her tongue before saying something she knew she'd regret later. She picked up the pace so they walked side by side. *Easier to go with it than fight.* Instead of arguing, she again pictured that large glass of chardonnay she planned to have later to wash away this stress.

At the corner of Elmwood and Main Street, a high school singing group decked out in white robes stood in a loose circle. Some of Chelsea's tension melted as the teens sang a carol about how things were beginning to look a lot like Christmas.

It was true. Every shop along Main Street was bright with strings of white holiday lights. Garlands and ribbons twirled around every streetlight and sign. The gathered crowd wore Santa hats and smiles on their faces. *Okay, so maybe being at a holiday stroll on a Friday night isn't the worst thing in the world.*

Her mother grabbed Chelsea's elbow again. "Let's go. I don't want them running out of any cookies before we get a chance to purchase them."

Chelsea sighed. So much for enjoying the Christmas spirit.

Paper bag luminarias lined the walkway up to the church hall, the candles quietly flickering in the cold air. The windows of the hall blazed with light. Music and crowd noises from inside seeped out into the night, mingling with the general cacophony of Main Street.

Before they reached the door, Martha cleared her throat. "To be clear, you are not to mention next weekend's event or the competition while we're inside. Is that understood?"

"Got it, Mom. I won't get in the way of your clandestine mission."

Martha frowned. "I don't think you're taking this seriously."

Chelsea yanked open the door, a blast of heat escaping into the night. "No, Mom, I'm not. It's a cookie competition, not life or death." She held the door and gestured for her mother to enter first.

"Well, we certainly won't win any trophies with *that* attitude." Martha passed her, untying her plaid wool scarf and shoving it into her coat pocket as she entered the warm building.

Chelsea closed her eyes and counted to ten before following her inside.

Her mother threaded a path through the crowd, ignoring the brightly colored displays of holiday items, and the smiling vendors standing behind their tables. Classic Christmas tunes wafted up to the rafters of the cavernous room, jingling bells and laughter filling the air, but Martha seemed oblivious to the holiday cheer as she pushed her way through the controlled chaos.

Chelsea huffed her annoyance. She could be home with her feet up right now, a large glass of wine in hand – except it wasn't her home, it was her mother's. Chelsea needed to pay off her debt and get a life of her own as soon as possible. Well, if this was going to be her last December on Cape Cod, she should make the most of it and at least enjoy the crafts and Christmas cheer filling the church hall.

She tapped her mother's arm to get her attention. "Mom, I'm going to look around at the vendor tables. Come find me when you're ready to leave."

The annoyance on Martha's face was obvious. "We are not here to shop. We're on a mission."

"*You're* the one on a mission, not me." Before her mother could react, Chelsea turned and walked away.

Grab your copy on AMAZON

EXCERPT FROM BATTLING BENJAMIN

PUBLISHED 2021 FROM WINDMILL POINT PUBLISHING

Elizabeth Watson loves her job. No, really. She enjoys being a realtor, helping people find their forever homes in the community she grew up in and cares about. When her family's business is purchased by a larger corporation she expects change. What she doesn't expect is the cocky, entitled heir-apparent taking over her life.

Benjamin Harrington is devastatingly handsome, with a sexy smirk and a sharp wit. He's also the most self-absorbed, arrogant man she's ever met, who hasn't worked a day in his charmed life. Personalities clash and sparks fly every time she's near him. He doesn't deserve to be her new boss.
Despite her best efforts, he invades her every thought... and dream. But what is it she wants? His job...or just him?

CHAPTER 1

One day. That's all he asked for.

One day to recover from the mess he found himself in.

"What were you thinking?"

His mother sat behind an imposing oak desk, hands clasped tightly in front of her atop a pile of listing folders. The windows of her Cambridge office revealed an impressive view of Harvard Square, bustling with life even on this cold, snowy morning. A view designed to impress clients. Impeccably coiffed blonde hair crowned her head like a battle helmet, her perfectly applied makeup like war paint. Even the brass buttons on her designer navy jacket were polished with Army precision.

Judith Harrington took real estate very, very seriously.

Unfortunately, Benjamin Harrington, her only son and heir apparent, did not. Selling homes was merely a job, not the cure to cancer. Negotiating sales between buyers and sellers was a game, not a hard fought battle. Ben didn't mind the few commercial real estate transactions he'd helped with. Those negotiations were true clashes between equals fighting for dominance, but all the rest of it?

Spending every weekend setting up and hosting open houses? The early mornings schlepping insipid buyers from property to property while nursing a hangover from the night before?

Not his thing.

"Benjamin Nathaniel Harrington, are you even listening to me?"

Uh oh, never a good sign when she pulls out the middle name. Ben sighed, realizing he'd tuned out her rant. He shifted his feet and clasped his hands behind his back. "Yes, Mom. I'm right here."

"But are you listening to me? Have you heard a single word I've said?" The fingers on her right hand now drummed a steady beat on the oak, the fingernails the exact shade of blood red to match her lipstick. The woman spent a lot of time crafting this perfect image, and marketing the hell out of it. Her face was plastered on brochures and billboards all across the state, wearing that same signature shade of lipstick, offsetting her unnaturally white smile. A smile that was conspicuously absent this morning.

"I apologized. I'm not sure what else you expect me to do."

"I *expect* you to act like a professional. For goodness sake, Benjamin, you're almost thirty years old. You should be settling down, not partying with your fraternity brothers every night of the week."

Ben frowned, crossing his arms over his chest. "What does my age have to do with anything?"

"You were passed out in the master bedroom, Benjamin. At your own open house. I need more of an explanation than 'I'm sorry.'" Her ice blue eyes narrowed as she stared at him expectantly.

He wasn't backing down, fighting the urge to scrub his fingers through his hair. "I wasn't passed out, I was tired. I was out late the night before celebrating New Year's Eve, like a normal person usually does. Who schedules an open house on New Year's Day at eight o'clock in the morning?"

"You need to grow up and get serious, Benjamin. Your father and I spent too long building this business to let it fall apart under your care. He would be so ashamed of your behavior."

Ben grimaced at the mention of his father. Nate Harrington was a legend in the world of Boston real estate. In little more than two decades, he built an empire of commercial and residential real estate offices across the state, all under the Harrington Realty World umbrella. Unfortunately, the long hours and stress took their toll. The year before, he suffered a heart attack while at his desk late one night. No one was around to call an ambulance, and by the time the cleaning crew found him it was too late.

Ben wasn't going to end up like his dad.

He wanted to enjoy life while he had the chance, not spend every minute tied to a desk or sitting at an open house smiling at strangers. And yeah, maybe he took things a little far over the last year. Too much drinking. Too many parties. But he was grieving, for fuck's sake.

To be fair, he hadn't meant to fall asleep at the open house. But the New Year's party he and his friends crashed at their old fraternity house was totally off the hook, not breaking up until well after dawn, which left him no time for actual sleep before he had to play host at his mother's ludicrously early open house.

"Maybe if you're going to plan events at the crack of dawn, you should plan to be there in person, *Mother*."

"And maybe I thought you were enough of an adult to handle this one on your own," she snapped back. "I see your father's faith in you was mistaken. You're clearly not ready to be an associate director at an office as busy as Cambridge."

Another pang of guilt ran through him, but Ben tried not to let his emotions show on his face. As much as he hated open houses, he hated the thought of disappointing his father even more. Maybe it had been irresponsible of him, and she was probably right. He could picture the frown on his father's face. *Damn.*

But better to pretend nothing fazed him than allow his mother to see how much her words hit the mark. He bit back his response and waited to see where she was going with this diatribe.

Judith Harrington always had an agenda.

When it was clear that he wasn't going to rise to her bait, she cleared her throat and took a folder from top of her inbox. "I think you need some time away from the city, and away from the bad influence of those friends of yours. I'm sending you to manage our new office acquisition, south of the city."

"For how long?"

She smirked and held out the folder, waving it at him until he reached for it. "Here's all the information on the office and the deals in progress for the next six months or so. Through the spring selling season at least. They'll expect you tomorrow morning."

Six months? Ben clutched the thick file and swallowed the angry words threatening to spew out. She might be his mother, and this might be particularly petty on her part to send him away without forewarning, but she still owned the company. He glanced at the folder's label. *Main Street, Chatham.* He inhaled and blew out a slow measured breath before replying in a low monotone. "Chatham? You've got to be joking."

"I assure you, I'm not. You can go to Chatham, or a rehab facility in the Berkshires. Your choice."

"But I've got a life here, Mother. Obligations to clients. Plans for the weekend. How will I be able to commute to Cape Cod every day?"

Her lips tipped up ever so slightly. "You won't. Cancel the plans and hand your listing books over to Miriam to get them redistributed. I need you there for Monday's morning meeting. Talk to Daniel about arrangements to stay in one of our rental properties in town." She pointed to the folder now in his hands. "Do your homework so you can hit the ground running. You're a Harrington and you need to start acting like one."

Acting like a Harrington? Ben bit his tongue to hold back any retort. What did that even mean? Unfeeling? Cold? Focused only on the bottom line? Only one thing was crystal clear.

He never wanted to be anything like his mother.

CHAPTER 2

One night. That's all she asked for.

One night where things went her way.

Well, some of the night wasn't so bad. The chardonnay was chilled to perfection. Candlelight danced and sparkled. The four piece jazz band tucked discretely into the far corner added just the right touch of ambience to the restaurant's upscale vibe. Chatham's Atlantic Coastal Inn boasted the romantic atmosphere for a perfect first date.

Well, almost perfect. But that wasn't the Inn's fault.

It was the date himself who was lacking.

Elizabeth Watson drew a deep breath and picked up her wine glass, twirling the golden liquid around the glass, reading the menu choices for the third time. At least Trey Dickerson knew how to choose a good bottle of wine.

"Hey, sorry about that, Elizabeth."

She glanced up as her date slipped back into the chair across from her. "Trey, I told you earlier. I prefer Eliza. Elizabeth sounds so formal."

Over his shoulder, she could see their server head toward the table. It was a slow January night, with few other patrons scattered around the huge dining room. In the last half hour, they'd only ordered a bottle of wine before Trey's phone rang and he walked out into the lobby to take the call.

Twenty minutes ago.

He'd said it was a quick business call about a closing the next day, which was a totally understandable excuse. But leaving your date sitting alone in a restaurant for twenty minutes? *Rude.*

"Is everything okay at the office?"

"What? Oh, sure. Anxious first-time buyers, you know how it goes. Airhead wife with a ton of stupid questions about every step along the way." He snorted a laugh. "As if she has any hope of understanding what's going on at the closing tomorrow."

Eliza wanted to correct the million things wrong with that blatantly sexist statement, but decided to settle on one. The most basic one, in her mind. "Isn't that your job as her realtor? To help her understand the process?"

Another snort laugh accompanied by a smirk. "You're too cute."

She glared.

The waiter cleared his throat. "Are you ready to order some appetizers? Or…"

Trey waved him off without even looking up. "I just sat down, for fuck's sake. Gimme some time to read the menu."

Eliza winced at the harshness of his tone. The server was young, maybe a college student, more likely still a senior in high school. She remembered her waitressing days and tried to lighten Trey's rude behavior with an apologetic smile. "We'll be ready to order in a minute."

"Very good." The waiter nodded and scurried off in retreat.

She glared at her date again, the angry look wasted since he now seemed fully engrossed in the menu. He looked just like his profile picture – tall, blond hair, chiseled cheekbones – but his entitled attitude left a lot to be desired. "You didn't have to be a dick to the waiter. He's just trying to do his job."

"Maybe he needs a different job."

"Maybe you should consider switching careers too. It doesn't sound like you explained the process very well if the buyers feel the need to call you in a panic the night before the closing."

He cocked his head. "Wait, are you serious? Elizabeth, I'm paid to be their realtor, not hold their hands. You're in the business, you know what I mean. These people have more money than sense."

"If you feel that way, why take them on as clients?"

He looked puzzled by the question. "It's my job, *Elizabeth*. I own the listing, they want the house. It's not like I have time in my day to be everyone's best buddy. I try to deal exclusively with high end second homes for people who know their way around a contract, but sometimes I get stuck with the fucking newbies."

She grimaced, but bit her tongue. She worked primarily as a buyer's broker and yes, she considered it her job to hold their hands and explain the process step-by-step when needed.

No point in getting into an argument over the right or wrong way to treat your clients. But… between the way he left her sitting alone for the first twenty minutes of their date – their first date, mind you – and his rude attitude toward the young waiter, Eliza already knew this would be the last time she went out on a date of any kind with this guy. They might live in the same town and have the same career, but they were too completely different to be compatible.

She took another large sip from her wineglass and then reached for the bottle. One more glass to bolster her morale. *Maybe it'll keep me from telling him off.* She decided she needed to pay her half of the dinner bill, and knew the Chicken Alfredo was the cheapest choice on the menu. No way did she want to feel she owed this prick anything in exchange for buying her meal.

Trey watched her pour more wine into the glass and smirked. "It's good, right? Not as buttery as the 2015 vintage, but very drinkable at fifty a bottle."

Fifty dollars? For chardonnay? She swallowed the sudden lump in her throat and told herself to breath. It's not like she didn't have the money in her account. It's just not the way she usually chose to spend it. She tried to squirrel away as much of her money as possible, saving for her dream house, even if it wasn't currently for sale. Ironic, since she was a realtor and saw hundreds of available properties each week, yet she'd fallen in love with a house she'd never even been inside of.

"I think we need another bottle." Trey swiveled his head to look for their server and snapped his fingers in the kid's direction.

Snapped. His. Fingers.

"Can we get a second bottle of this? My date needs another drink. Stat."

"Trey, we don't need more wine. We haven't even eaten anything yet." She pushed the wine glass a little further out of reach. Maybe she was drinking it too fast. "Aren't you hungry?"

"Starved." He leaned across the table and leered at her. "We could always skip the entrée and go straight to the *dessert* portion of our evening."

He obviously wasn't talking about the Inn's famous chocolate lava cake. Her gut churned at the thought of him putting his mouth anywhere near hers, let alone any other body parts getting involved. "I think you're getting a little ahead of yourself."

He sat back in his chair and narrowed his eyes. "Listen, Elizabeth. You're young. You're cute. And you may be the top seller in your little office, but if you want to take your sales game to the next level, you need a guy like me in your corner pulling the strings."

Her eyebrows shot up. "Excuse me?"

He chuckled. "We both know there's more going on here than a simple boy-meets-girl on a dating app kind of thing. You want to jump ship from your dinky little office and come work with the big boys."

"Are you insulting my mother's business?"

He cocked his head. "Your mother was smart, selling off to Harrington Realty while the market was hot last year. But you must have noticed that all the good earners are leaving, going elsewhere. You swiped right on me because of my professional connections. I respect that. But I'm not gonna hand them over without a little quid pro quo. You suck mine and I'll suck yours, that sorta thing."

What. The. Fuck?

The waiter returned with the second bottle of chardonnay, a white cloth draped over his arm to present the bottle.

"Don't uncork that," Eliza told him holding out one hand like a stop sign. She grabbed her wallet from her purse and snagged a credit card. "Please put the first bottle on this and close our tab. We won't be staying for dinner."

Trey smirked at her. "Don't be such a haughty ice princess, Elizabeth. You think you're all that because you were top seller in mommy's office, but that's over now. You're not real estate royalty anymore."

"I never said I was," she shot back.

"Then stay and eat dinner with me. Discuss our new business arrangement over dinner."

She looked him in the eye, her anger on a tight leash. "There won't be any arrangement. I don't do business with slime balls."

"You're being unreasonable."

"And you're being a complete jerk."

He stood and slammed his napkin down on the table, rattling the silverware. "Fine. But don't you dare come crawling to me later when you want to cut a deal."

She snorted at the ridiculousness of his statement. "No worries there."

He opened his mouth as if to say something more, but closed it and stalked out of the restaurant.

She watched him leave, breathing a sigh of relief. *How did that go so horribly wrong in so little time?* She closed her eyes and took a few deep, cleansing breaths.

When she opened them again, a redheaded woman wearing a chef's coat sat in the chair Trey recently vacated.

Eliza swallowed and tried to smile, but knew it probably looked more like a grimace. "Hey, Abbie."

"I hear we have some trouble in the dining room."

She cringed. Abbie Duncan worked as the Inn's head chef, so their waiter must have gone running back to the kitchen to share the details of her disastrous date. Doubly embarrassing since she'd known

Abbie since high school. They'd been on the cheer squad together and they had a lot of friends in common. More recently, she'd helped Abbie and her fiancé buy a new home overlooking Nantucket Sound. Not that chefs in Chatham typically earned enough to buy waterfront property, but Jake came from Old Boston money.

"No trouble. Just a misunderstanding of sorts."

Abbie cocked her head to one side. "Yeah? What sort would that be?"

"The sort where he thought dinner included an automatic blowjob on the first date. I disagreed." She didn't want to get into the whole business deal side of the argument.

Abbie grimaced. "Ouch. That sucks."

"Well, more accurately, there will be no sucking involved."

"Good one." Abbie extended her palm and waited for Eliza to high five her. "Don't leave me hanging here."

"I'm not sure a failed first date is really high five worthy." But she tapped her hand to Abbie's nonetheless. "Sorry we made a scene in your restaurant. Shouldn't you be in the kitchen doing your thing?"

Abbie shrugged. "It's a slow night. Actually, when Fred told me a patron snapped his fingers at him I had to come out here. Nobody pulls that shit with my staff and gets away with it, not even in the height of the season. I don't care if he's the prince of England. It's rude and uncalled for."

Laughter bubbled up from Eliza's gut. "That's Trey Dickerson to a tee. Rude and uncalled for."

Her friend laughed along before pushing the chair back to stand. "You should stay. Have some dinner."

As she was speaking, the waiter arrived with the bill for the over-priced wine.

Eliza shook her head and reached for the check. "I've got an early meeting tomorrow morning. I should get home."

"Let me take care of this for you." The other woman plucked the bill from the waiter's hand. "You shouldn't get stuck with paying for a bad date."

While she wanted to protest, Eliza knew it wasn't a big deal for Abbie to comp the bottle of chardonnay. "Thanks. I appreciate it."

"No problem at all. And hey, don't let one bad date get you down."

She gave her friend a wry smile. "Sometimes it feels like all the good ones are already taken."

"I thought that too, before I met Jake. You just haven't met the right guy."

"When Trey's picture popped up as a match on the app, I thought maybe this was it. He checked all the boxes on my list, plus he grew up on the Cape." Eliza sighed. She pushed back her chair and slid on her winter coat, following Abbie out of the main dining room. "I'm in my mid-twenties and still looking for a unicorn."

"You mean, you're looking for your lobster," Abbie said with a smile. "You want a Cape Cod guy, right? And don't they say lobsters mate for life?"

Eliza laughed. "You know that's not true. It's a myth perpetuated by viral sitcom clips. Male lobsters are some of the most promiscuous creatures in the sea."

Abbie held up both hands. "I'm not a marine biologist. I just cook the damn things."

"And on that note, I'll say thank you and good night."

"But seriously, Eliza." Abbie touched her arm. "He's out there. Your unicorn. Maybe you need to rethink some of those checkboxes on your list."

She smiled. "Probably. And I definitely need to stop dating lobsters."

Grab your copy on AMAZON

ABOUT THE AUTHOR

Katie O'Sullivan is an award-winning author with more than a dozen books to her credit, many of which are available in paperback (great for stocking stuffers) including *My Kind of Crazy, Ghost In the Machine, Once Upon a Christmas Cookie*, and the *Son of a Mermaid* series for young teen readers (and anyone else who loves mermaids.)

A recovering English major, she earned her degree at Colgate University and now lives on Cape Cod with her family and big dogs, drinking way too much coffee and finding new uses for all the sea glass she collects from the beach up the road. She also posts an obsessive number of dog pictures on Instagram because she can't help herself. (Do you have a dog? Then you understand.) She writes YA and romantic suspense novels, as well as working full time for a high-tech company based in California (big hooray for working remotely!), pretending to be in charge of a large, exuberant team of proposal writers. Which may explain all the coffee...

Check out her website at www.katie-osullivan.com

facebook.com/AuthorKatieOSullivan
instagram.com/capecodkatie
amazon.com/Katie-OSullivan/e/B0039VWSD4